In Enemy Territory

M.E. Clayton

ISBN: 9780463858318

DEDICATION

For My Grandsons-
One day, you will all meet a girl who will shine so brightly that she'll cast away all the shadows that threaten to drag you down. Your job is to make sure you give her everything she needs to keep shining. Her lightness will diminish your darkness. I love you boys.

CONTENTS

ACKNOWLEDGMENTS

The first acknowledgment will always be my husband. There aren't enough words to express my gratitude for having this man in my life. There is a little bit of him in every hero I dream up, and I can't thank God enough for bringing him into my life. Thirty years, and still going strong!

Second, there's my family; my daughter, my son, my grandchildren, my sister, and my mother. Family is everything, and I have one of the best. They are truly the best cheerleaders I could ever ask for, and I never forget just how truly blessed I am to have them in my life.

And, of course, there's Kamala. This woman is not only my beta and idea guinea pig, but she's also one of my closest friends. She's been with me from the beginning of this journey, and we're going to ride this thing to the end. Kam's the encouragement that sparked it all, folks.

And, finally, I'd like to thank everyone who's purchased, read, reviewed, shared, and supported me and my writing. Thank you so much for helping make this dream a reality and a happy, fun one at that! I cannot say thank you enough.

PROLOGUE

Fiona – (Five-Years-Old) ~

I don't think he likes me.

The boy with the black hair keeps looking at me like Daddy does when he's yelling at Momma. Is he mad at me because I got the bucket of crayons first? I'll share if he wants to color, too. Momma is always telling me that people should share, so I'll share if he wants.

Is he sitting in the corner because Miss Julie got him in trouble? Maybe that's why he looks mad, and he really does like me.

Should I take him some crayons? Will Miss Julie get mad at me if I do? All the other kids are playing and having fun, so maybe she won't get mad. I know, I'll ask her first. If the black-haired boy is in trouble, then Miss Julie will tell me.

She's picking up the read time books from our group table. I tug on her skirt, so she will look at me. "Miss Julie?" She looks down at me and smiles. Miss Julie is very pretty. She has soft, yellow hair, and she's always putting flowers in it. Her eyes are blue, and she is always laughing. She's also very nice to me. I'm happy that Momma made her my teacher.

"Hey, Fiona."

"Is it okay if I share the crayons with the boy in the corner?" I whispered.

I guess she didn't hear me because she bends her knees, so I don't have to look up anymore. "I'm sorry, Fiona, I didn't hear you."

I looked over at the boy really fast. He's still looks like he's mad, so I looked back at Miss Julie. "Is the boy in the corner in time-out? I think he wants to color."

Miss Julie looked over at the boy, and then she looked at me again. "No, sweetie, he's not in trouble. He…uh…he just likes to play by himself sometimes."

Oh, good. He wasn't in trouble. "So, he can color if he wants?"

Miss Julie started biting on her lower lip and I wonder if it hurts when she does that. "Y…yes, Fiona. He can color if he wants to."

I ran to pick up the colors I was using. After I put them all back in the bucket, I grabbed two color books, then carried them over to the black-haired boy.

Hopefully, he would see that I was nice, and he'd want to be my friend. Momma says it's good to have lots of friends. It means you'll never be alone if you have lots of friends. I already had my new friend named Victoria, but it was okay if we had more friends.

The boy didn't say anything as I put the crayons and coloring books on the floor in front of him. He still looked mad, but once I tell him I'll share the crayons, I know he'll be happy.

"Hi. My name is Fiona." I smiled at him because Momma says my smile makes people happy, and I wanted my new friend to be happy.

He didn't tell me his name, though. He just sat there, still looking mad.

I know! He didn't know that I was sharing the crayons, so that's why he was still mad. "I brought you a color book. It's a boy color book, and it's okay if you want to use the crayons. I'll share and we can color together."

He closed his green eyes. I've never seen green eyes before. Momma's and Daddy's eyes are brown, so my eyes are brown. I've seen blue eyes, like Miss Julie's, but I've never seen green eyes. They were very pretty.

When he opened his eyes, he finally talked to me. "Why are you talking to me?"

Didn't he know that we were going to be friends? "Because I want you to be my friend," I told him. "I'm Fiona. What's your name?"

"I don't want to be your friend, so leave me alone, Fiona."

My nose started to tickle like when I'm going to start to cry. "Why don't you want to be my friend? I'll be a nice friend, I promise."

"I don't want to be your friend because I'm not friends with stupid girls."

He was a meanie. "I'm not stupid!"

"Yes, you are! My friends make me feel happy. You just make me feel weird."

I can't believe how mean he's being to me. "What do I make you feel?" I asked.

He leaned into my face. "You make me feel like the bad guys on Halloween."

He stood up, and walking away, he didn't care that he had left me crying here.

CHAPTER 1

Is he my friend, or isn't he?

Fiona – (Ten-Years-Old) ~

I couldn't wait to see Vicky. She wasn't on the school bus this morning, so she was probably running late as usual. I jumped off the bus so excited to find her and show her my new art bag that I actually, rudely, pushed some kids aside as I hopped off the last step of the bus door opening.

I would always hear my parents fighting about not having enough money to pay bills and stuff, so last night when my mom told me she had been saving a little bit, here and there, to buy me this bag, I had been so overwhelmed with gratitude that I couldn't stop the tears. It hadn't been my birthday or Christmas, so I had been a little confused over why she had gotten me the bag, but I'd been too happy to ask any questions.

The bag was an oversized tote with a million pockets on the inside to hold all my art supplies. It was also dark blue with a hundred different lighter shades of blue slashed throughout the material. And since blue was my favorite color, that made the bag just that much more awesome.

I finally made my way through the school's front doors. Vicky and I went to Hamilton Elementary in Smithtown, California. It was one of those schools where everything was inside one big building. There was another elementary school on the other side of town, but that one was open everywhere. I wished I could go there instead. It seemed nice to be able to leave class and walk directly outside into the sun, rain, or whatever. It didn't have that cooped-up vibe that Hamilton had.

I only had ten minutes before the bell rang, so I could only blame my uncontrollable excitement for what happened next. I was usually very good about paying attention to who all were roaming up and down the hallways. I've had my share of embarrassing run-ins and I tried to avoid being in the spotlight as much as possible. However, the excitement over my new art bag had overshadowed common self-preservation because I didn't see the dark-haired, green-eyed boy in front of me until my front was brought to hard stop by his back.

I wish I had been paying better attention. I wish I had been quick enough to recognize him and take off running the other way. I wish I had done a lot of things differently, but I hadn't. Damien whirled around in a flurry of green, and I instantly took a step back and clutched my backpack and new art bag to my body.

He was wearing his green jacket over a simple white t-shirt, a pair of blue jeans, and a pair of white sneakers. His dark hair was shaggy around his face and his green eyes were, as always, looking at me with hate. I had no idea what I ever did to this boy to make him dislike me so much, but he did. He also made no effort to pretend otherwise. "Are you blind or something?" His friends snickered next to him.

I shook my head. "N…no. I'm sorry." Now here's the part where I should either turn around and go back the way I came or sidestep him and his friends, then rush past them, but I did neither of those things.

Damien Sebastian Greystone III has been nothing but mean to me since we were five-years-old. And because he's been mean to me for so long, I knew that no matter which way I moved, he was going to do or say something to embarrass me. So, on the too-many-occasions-to-count when I was around him, I stood still and took it until he was done with whatever form of torture he chose to inflict.

The only good thing I could say was that I was proud that, no matter how mean he was to me, I always looked him in the eye. Damien scared me, and he hurt my feelings all the time, but I always looked him in his eerie green eyes when he did. I hid from him a lot, but when I couldn't, I tried to be ready.

He looked at my hair, then my face, and then my clothes. He always got an ugly look on his face whenever he looked at my shoes, though. I wasn't sure why he hated my shoes, but I also didn't know why he hated me, either. "What's that?"

I froze.

Absolutely froze.

He was talking about my new art bag.

I started shaking my head so hard that I could feel the little butterfly clips Momma put in my hair this morning coming loose. I hugged the bag closer to my chest. "No…nothing."

The corner of his lip went up like he might smile, but I knew better. He never smiled at me. *Ever.* "Are you lying to me?"

Yes! "It's just the new art bag my momma bought me."

He reached his arm out towards me. "Let me see it."

I could feel the tingle in my nose again that warned me I was about to cry. "W...why?"

He took a step closer towards me and I could hear his friends start 'oohing' at me. "I said let me see it, Halloween."

"No. I…I have to get to class." I held the bag even tighter.

I was so shocked when he just nodded his head and stepped aside, so I could pass him. I looked down the hall, and I saw Vicky coming my way. I was so happy to see her that I smiled and rushed forward to meet her. I had just made it past Damien when I felt a rush of air as my new bag was pulled out of my hands.

Stupid! Stupid! Stupid!

I should have held on tighter until I had made it to class.

I turned around and saw my new art bag in Damien's hands. I couldn't stop the tears because I already knew what was going to happen next. "Damien, pl…please…give me back my bag. *Please.*"

He looked at his friends. "Awe…she wants her bag back. What do you guys think? Should I give her the bag?"

I could see Vicky standing next to me now. "I'm going to tell the teacher if you don't give Fiona back her bag, Damien!"

Damien gave Vicky the same look he always gave my shoes. "Sure thing, Vicky."

I held my breath. It wasn't going to be that easy. It never was with him.

I reached out to take my bag back, but before I could get my hands on it, Damien had taken both his hands and tugged down the seams, ripping the bag in half.

It felt like there was someone really heavy sitting on my lungs as I watched him throw the bag at my feet. "That's what happens when your mom buys you cheap things, Halloween. They fall apart."

The bell for class rang and everyone around me started scattering to get to class while I stood there crying over my bag. I could feel Vicky's arms around me as I cried.

I hated Damien Greystone, no matter how much Jesus said we shouldn't hate people. I hated him. *Absolutely hated him.*

When I got home from school, I had lied to Momma and told her that I left my new art bag at school. I lied again and had told her I did it because I was scared of losing it on the bus. She believed me because she didn't think that I lied, and I usually didn't. The only time I lied was whenever Damien did something to me. I wasn't sure why I lied, but I did. He was so mean to me, but I was scared to get him in trouble. If he was this mean to me when I haven't done anything to him, I didn't want to know what he'd do to me if I *did* do something to cause him trouble.

I cried myself to sleep that night and the next day at school I made sure I stayed away from Damien. And because I ran to class, I was the first one there. My teacher, Mrs. Bicksley, just smiled at me as I went to my desk. I sat in the back of the room because it was safest. Damien sat two rows ahead of me, and so I felt better knowing I could watch him.

My feet slowed down as I walked to my desk. Our desks were given to us when school started and no one else sat in them but us, so I was surprised to see something peeking out from my desk chair.

I finally got to my seat and I started to panic.

In my chair was a dark blue art bag. It looked brand-new.

I stood there afraid to touch it.

After a minute or so, I noticed a little white tag on one of the many zippers. I reached over to check it out. It might have someone's name on it because there's no way this could be for me. I turned the tag over and saw that it was a price tag. My nose started to tingle again.

The bag cost $150.00!

I put my backpack on top of my desk and picked up the bag to look at it. It was such a pretty art bag. It felt thicker than the one Momma had bought me and there were fancy pockets on the outside of this one. It also felt heavier. I pulled on the main zipper to look inside and I couldn't stop my panicked breathing. Inside the bag were brand-new art supplies. I could see colored pencils, new chalks in so many different colors, and two art pads.

I dug inside to look for a card or something to tell me that this bag was really mine. Maybe Vicky got it for me. Maybe she told Mrs. Bicksley, and Mrs. Bicksley felt so bad that she bought it for me because it couldn't be from…no…*could it?*

I looked up as the kids in my class started coming inside. The second that I saw Damien walk in the room, I dropped the bag back into my seat. I didn't want him to see it. I didn't want him to rip it from my hands and destroy it again.

It wasn't until we were the only ones still standing in the class that I saw his green eyes jump to the bag and then back to me. He stared at me until Mrs. Bicksley told us to take a seat and it wasn't until he turned his back that I could finally breathe.

I also knew who the bag was from.

CHAPTER 2

He's NOT my friend.

Fiona – (Thirteen-Years-Old) ~

I was so nervous.

Vicky was trying to act like a cool teenager, but I knew she was just as nervous as I was. We were at our first 8th-grade nighttime school dance and I kept going back and forth from nervous to excited.

Vicky was lucky. She had a sort-of-boyfriend already. Tommy Granger had begun paying special attention to her after we had gotten back from Christmas break. It had started out with him walking her to her classes, and then they started texting a lot. She said she's not officially his girlfriend because he hasn't asked her yet, but I was pretty sure it was just a matter of time before he did.

He was also very cute. He was tall, but to be fair, I was only five-two, so he might just be tall to me. He had blonde hair and the kindest blue eyes I've ever seen. He played on the football team, and he was pretty smart from what I could see of the few classes we had together. I was so happy for my friend. A girl could do a lot worse than Tommy Granger.

"How do I look?" Vicky asked me for the twentieth time.

"You look gorgeous, Vee." She really did, and I wasn't just saying that because she was my friend. Vicky really was a pretty girl. She was the same height as I was, but instead of possessing the same boring brown hair and brown eyes that I did, she had stunning red hair-not orange, but real red-and sharp hazel eyes. She played soccer and basketball, so her figure was slim and athletic. She was a true beauty inside and out and the best person I knew.

She was dressed in a deep green summer dress with tan strap-wrapping sandals. Her red hair was loose around her shoulders and her face was completely makeup-free. Vicky didn't need makeup, even if she did hate the light spatter of freckles across her nose.

We were sitting at one of the tables closest to the gym exit. It was far away enough from the DJ that we could hear each other over the music, but it also provided a quick route to the restrooms. There were a couple of classmates of ours sitting with us, Sarah and Juanita, and while we didn't super hang out or anything, we were still all cool with each other.

I noticed Vicky biting her lip. "What's wrong, Vee?"

She leaned into me in an attempt at privacy. "I think Tommy might try to kiss me tonight."

My eyes widened. If he did, it would be her first real kiss. "Oh. My. God. What makes you think that?"

She shrugged a dainty shoulder. "I don't know. It's just a feeling. He's been getting more affectionate lately. I don't know."

"Wow. That's just…wow." I could admit I was kind of envious. I wasn't boy crazy or anything like that, but we were already in the 8th grade and no boys had ever shown any kind of interest in hanging out with me. I wasn't rich or anything special to look at, so it wasn't like I expected boys to be lined out the door to date me. Still, one guy would be nice.

"I'm so anxious, Fee. What if I'm a bad kisser? Or what if it's a boring first kiss? *Ugh,"* she groaned in frustration.

"No way, Vee. You're going to be an awesome kisser. You're good at everything you do, so this will be no different." I reached over and squeezed her arm. "I promise."

I could see a shadow clouding over me, and I turned, then looked up to see Phillip Jansen standing above me. "Hey, Fiona." He darted a look over at Vicky. "Vic."

Phillip has always been nice to me, if not a little reserved. "Hey, Phillip."

He started tapping his feet like he was nervous or something. "Yeah, I was just…uh, wondering if you'd like to dance, Fee?"

My heart started racing in my chest. The music the DJ had on was slow, so that meant we'd be dancing close together.

Suddenly, I felt inferior. I had chosen to wear a light blue, short-sleeved blouse that fit loosely around my torso. I was developing faster and larger than I would have liked around my chest and hip areas, so I did my best to choose clothing that slimmed my body some. I didn't like being fat. Momma called it curvy, but everyone else in the world called it fat. I had matched it to a light pair of jeans and the best sneakers I had. Momma had helped me put my hair up in a fancy clip that let random curls hang loose here and there. I wasn't old enough to wear makeup, so there wasn't anything I could do about that. Still, Phillip looked super nice, though. A little too nice for me, in my opinion.

I didn't realize he had his hand held out to me until Vicky kicked me in my shin. I jumped up and took his hand. "Yes…uh, yeah…yup. I mean…" *Oh, Good Lord.* "Yes, Phillip, I'd love to dance with you."

We were walking out onto the dance floor together and, I swear, he had to be able to feel my palms sweating. I wasn't nervous because this was my first dance with a boy. I was nervous at the thought that maybe, *finally,* a boy might like me.

We got to the dance floor and he put his arms around me like the other boys on the dance floor had around their dancing partners. I studied the girls, and so it looked like I should have my arms around Phillip's neck. We danced like this for a little bit, and it was nice.

I should have known it wasn't going to last.

A couple of minutes into our dance, I felt myself being wrenched out of Phillip's arms. I stumbled backwards as I tried to grab my bearings, and I would have fallen if not for the hand holding my arm in a steel vise grip. I was so confused as I tried to yank myself free from the grip, but it wasn't until I heard *that voice* that I knew this was going to be bad.

"Am I interrupting?" Damien's voice was all razor-sharp edges. I'd been on the receiving end of his insults and taunts for years, but I don't think I've ever heard his voice come out so menacing.

To his credit, Phillip didn't back down. "Yeah, you are, Greystone. Fiona and I are in the middle of a dance."

Damien finally turned his attention towards me, and I withered inside a little. It wasn't fair that he was so gorgeous. His family had a lot of money, so he was always dressed in the latest brand-name styles. Still, I had a feeling he'd look just as good in rags as he did in designer clothes.

Tonight, he was dressed in a light blue button-up shirt and dark blue jeans. He had his signature Nikes on, but instead of the matching baseball hat he favored, he let his jet-black hair fall back from his beautifully evil face.

Damien was rarely seen alone, so like every other time I've seen him, he had his cronies with him. "Is that so, Jansen?"

Phillip nodded. "Yeah, so if you don't mind-"

"Ahhh, but here's the thing, Jansen, I *do* mind," Damien slithered out.

What? How? Where? What? Why in the heck would Damien mind?

"See, Jansen, we're teammates and teammates depend on each other. What kind of team captain would I be if I let one of my teammates get cozy with a girl who has already fucked her virginity away at the age of thirteen?"

I gasped in shock as Phillip shot me an incredulous look. "You're lying!" I shouted.

Damien shook me using the hold he had on my arm. "If I were you, I'd shut the hell up right now," he growled, and I should. I probably really, really should, but...

I shook my head and pleaded with Phillip to believe me. "Phillip, he's lying. I've never even kissed a boy yet. *He's lying.*"

He looked like he wanted to believe me, but I didn't know if he was strong enough to go up against Damien. "It's just a dance, Damien. It doesn't mean anything."

My heart crumbled at his words. I had been so excited to think that he might like me, but his words made it perfectly clear that he was just after a harmless dance.

Damien kept stepping to Phillip until he was right up in his face. "Then dance with another girl if she doesn't mean anything to you. You'll be safer for it, Jansen."

Phillip's eyes darted towards me. "Sorry, Fee," he mumbled. He walked off the dance floor, leaving me in the middle of Damien and his posse. I tried to wrench my arm away again, but instead, I was hauled out through the side exit.

Damien was practically dragging me down the hallway. Once we were fairly far away from the gym, Damien swung me around, slamming my back up against the lockers, and I was petrified.

He placed his hands on either side of my shoulders, effectively blocking an exit. I'd never seen his stare hold so much loathing and hate before. He looked like he wanted to strangle me.

It was a full two minutes before he spoke and said, "You're going to stay away from Jansen or-"

"What?!" I yelled. "You can't tell me who I can be friends with, Damien!"

He leaned in so close that I had to tilt my head back to look at him. "You're going to stay away from Jansen or else, if you don't, I will make it my personal mission to let every boy in school know you're nothing but a dirty, used up slut."

I stood there in absolute horror as he pushed back from the lockers and walked away.

CHAPTER 3

But only friends do that, right?

Fiona – (Sixteen-Years-Old) ~

I knew this party was a bad idea. The only reason we were here was because Vicky had heard that her newest crush was going to be here.

I very rarely went to any high school parties because odds were that Damien would be there. I got enough torture and torment from him during school hours that I didn't need to go looking for it off the clock.

I'd like to say Vicky had guilt tripped me into coming to Ryland Obermen's party, but she hadn't. Vicky has been my best friend since kindergarten, and in all these years, her loyalty has never wavered. She's missed out on a lot of school parties and functions just to sit at home with me and keep me company. So, when she had wanted to come to this party, hoping to hook up with Ben Lester, I had pretended to be excited about attending.

But with all my heart and soul, I didn't want to be here.

"Are you sure you're okay with being here, Fee?"

I waved away her concerns. "Yeah, Vee. We're juniors in high school. We need to start doing things like this more often."

She grabbed my arms, and using them as leverage, started jumping up and down. "Yay! Let's mingle and see if he's here yet."

We wandered through the house and randomly chatted with people we knew. It wasn't until we had made our way to the backyard that we found Ben. He was drinking and hanging out by the pool.

Vicky turned towards me. "Okay, he's here. Let's go over and talk to him."

I wanted to say yes so badly, but only because I felt out of my element. I really didn't want to ruin her chances with Ben, though. "You go ahead. I need to find a bathroom in this place."

She eyed me like she knew I was bullshitting her. "Are you sure? We can find the bathroom first, and then go talk to Ben."

I shook my head. "I'll be fine, Vee." I smacked her on her ass. "Go get your man." I laughed for good measure. Vicky would never leave me if she knew I was feeling nervous. *Never.*

I waited until she was standing in front of Ben before I went in search of the bathroom. I didn't really need to use it, though. I was just hoping I could hide in it for a bit.

I made my way up the spiral staircase on the left side of the living room and wandered the halls. The party was looking to be a typical unchaperoned teenage party. There were drugs, alcohol, and rated PG-13 nudity everywhere.

I was halfway down the hallway when I was suddenly grabbed by some drunk guy coming out of one of the bedrooms. Before I could make out who the boy was, he had cradled my face in his hands and started kissing me.

I let out a shocked gasp, and he used that opportunity to slip his tongue inside my mouth.

Holy lips and tongue, Batman! This was my first kiss ever!

I was kissing a boy. Could you believe it? *Me.* Short, plump, brown-haired, brown-eyed Fiona Eldstead was being kissed-*finally.*

I was enjoying the kiss so much that I didn't take notice of his hand moving down over my hip at first. I reached down to bring his hand back up, but he wasn't having it. This boy-whose name I didn't even know-suddenly grabbed my hips and yanked me towards him, and while I may have never been kissed before, I knew exactly what it was that was rubbing up against my body.

I turned my head away from his kiss and began pushing at his shoulders. "Stop it."

He must not have heard me because he started kissing my neck and rubbing himself faster on my hip. "I said, stop it! Please, let me go!"

He heard me that time. "Awe, c'mon, sweetheart. You don't really want me to stop."

I did.

I really, really did want him to stop.

I pushed at his shoulders as hard as I could, but he wouldn't budge. I started to panic. "Stop it! Now! Get off me!"

"Listen-" He didn't get to finish what he was going to say.

One second, he was on me, then the next thing I knew, he was being thrown to the floor and Damien Greystone was over him, punching the boy…well…everywhere. The sight was enough to paralyze me. I wondered what this kid had done to piss off Damien like that.

I stood there in shock because, let's be honest, I didn't know what people were supposed to do when something like this happened at these parties. It wasn't until Damien's sidekicks, William Creston and Jake Everol, stepped in that Damien was pulled off of the guy.

"Dame, dude-" William began, but Damien ignored him.

Damien turned towards me and I was positive that I had never seen anything so magnificent in all my sixteen years of living. His chest was heaving, his balled-up fists were bloody, and his eyes were blazing in green flames. He was so beautiful that, in this moment, it actually hurt my heart that he hated me so much.

There were all kinds of chaos around us, but all I could focus on was him. I guess he felt the same because, the next thing I knew, he was pulling me into the room closest to us. He literally threw me inside and slammed the door shut behind him.

The room was dark, but there was enough light coming in through the window from the streetlight outside to make each other out. I stayed quiet, waiting for him to say something. I had never seen him like this, and while I didn't think he'd ever hit me, I honestly wasn't sure. So, I waited silently like a coward.

It didn't take long before he let out a roar and started punching the wall. I stood there stunned at his violence. It wasn't until I could actually see holes covered in blood decorating the wall that I moved.

I rushed towards him and grabbed his arm in the middle of another throw. "Damien, stop it!"

He rounded on me and the look on his face had me running for the door. Unfortunately for me, he got there before I could turn the knob. He swung me around and his grip on my shoulders was so tight that I whimpered. He was going to leave bruises. I looked up as he towered over me, and I was truly afraid. "Please don't hurt me-"

His brows drew inward. "Hurt you? You think I'm going to *hurt* you?"

I shook my head because, frankly, I didn't know what to think. "I don't know," I whispered.

"*How could you let him kiss you?*" he snarled.

What?

"I...I...didn't. It...it wasn't like that."

He leaned in closer if that was even possible. "Then explain to me how it *was*, Halloween?"

"I...I was looking for the bathroom. H...he came out of one of the rooms, grabbed me, and then just started kissing me." I thought it was best for my well-being to leave out how I had briefly kissed him back.

"Oh, really?" Damien was searching my face for the lie.

"I tried to push him away," I whispered.

I could see Damien's jaw flex from grinding his teeth. "Did he hurt you?"

I shook my head quickly for fear that Damien would go back outside and kill him. "No. You stopped him before he could do anything serious." And then a thought occurred to me. "H...how did you know it was me? How did you find me?"

Unbelievably, the look on his face now was more terrifying than when he had been beating that kid. "I always know where you're at, Halloween," he replied, his voice like silk pouring out of his lips.

I don't know what possessed me to confess to him, but I did. "That was my first kiss." I let out a small, sad laugh. "It's not what I always thought it'd be."

Damien snapped out, "That is *not* your first kiss, Fiona."

Fiona? He never called me Fiona. If he had to address me, it was always Halloween.

"Dam-" I was interrupted by Damien's lips crashing down on mine.

Holy Mary, Mother of God, Damien Greystone was kissing me.

Even though the entire thing had been a disaster, I was so grateful for the kiss earlier because now I had an idea of what to expect and what I should do. I wrapped my fists in his shirt and hesitantly opened my mouth to welcome him in.

I felt a rumble erupt from his throat as his tongue swept in to dance with mine. He tasted like mint and alcohol. He tasted absolutely delicious.

He wrapped both his hands in my hair, and the deeper the kiss became, the tighter his grip pulled. Too soon, it was all over, and he was pulling back from me. "*That* was your first."

Damien stepped away from me, then reaching around me to open the door, effectively dismissing me, he said, "When you leave this room, find Vicky and go the fuck home. If I find you're still here later, it won't end well for you." He walked out of the room leaving me standing alone, cold and confused.

I touched my lips with my fingertips, wondering if the kiss had even happened. Why would Damien Greystone save me? Why would he *kiss* me?

More importantly, how could I let him? This boy has been nothing but horrible to me for over ten years, but his kiss was the best thing I had ever felt in my life.

What the hell was wrong with me?

CHAPTER 4

He, most definitely, *isn't my friend.*

Fiona – (Eighteen-Years-Old) ~

I was such a loser. It was just past midnight on graduation night, and I was already in bed. I had left an epic party at Vicky's on-again-off-again boyfriend's house just to come home. She and Ben had been going back and forth since the night she got her hooks into him at Ryland's party.

The same night Damien had kissed me.

I wish I could say things had become easier between us after that night, but they hadn't. In fact, they had gotten worse. He wasn't meaner towards me, just...colder. He had also started going through girls like he was trying to break a world record. Admittedly, I never saw him kiss or touch anyone, but there was always some random girl hanging on him.

Always.

As the pathetic train that was my life kept going, that was the reason I was home instead of at the party. Damien had shown up at the party, and he hadn't shown up alone. Heather Winston had been with him and seeing her hug and kiss on him had done strange things to me. I had felt jealous and confused.

I knew Damien hated me, but his singular efforts to torment me all these years had somehow made me feel special to him. Intellectually, I knew I wasn't, but after that kiss last year, my emotions had been looking for his torture to mean something.

I was such a dweeb; the dweebest of all dweebs.

I was surprised when I heard tapping on my window. I wasn't scared or worried since it could only be Vicky. She had told her parents that she was spending the night with me, when in actuality, she had made plans to spend the night with Ben. They had started having sex a couple of months ago and now they created opportunities when they could. They must have gotten into a fight and were off-again.

I got up and padded my way to the window. I pulled the blinds up and it wasn't my red-haired, freckled-face best friend I was looking at.

It was Damien Greystone.

What in the ever-lovin' hell?

I opened the window out of shock more than anything else. "What are you doing here?"

He didn't answer me. He just placed his hands on the window ledge and hauled himself over. I stepped back still in a little bit of shock at seeing Damien Greystone entering my bedroom through the window. "Why aren't you at Ben's party?" I tried again to find out what he was doing here.

It wasn't until I noticed his green gaze leave my face and journey downward that I remembered I was only wearing my nighttime blue tank top and a pair of white lace panties. To be fair, I had never imagined in a million years that Damien would be in my bedroom tonight when I had gotten ready for bed earlier. Never having been a confident girl, my first instinct was to cover myself up, but he had already seen me in all my big boobs, wide hips, and thick thighs glory, so what was the point?

Besides, I wasn't confused about what he thought about me. My body wasn't going to make a difference in how he saw me or felt about me.

"Why'd you leave the party?" he asked.

I shrugged a shoulder. "I was bored." I'd never tell him the truth.

He kept walking until he was directly in front of me. With each step, I had to lean my head back to keep his face in my line of sight. Damien was well over six-feet tall now and playing sports had molded his body into a work of art. He may hate me, and I may despise him, but I wasn't blind.

My entire being froze in astonishment and disbelief when Damien reached out and ran his hand, every so softly, down my neck, over my collarbone, then down to my breast. I stood mannequin-still as he held the weight of my breast in his hand and began running his thumb back and forth over the nipple.

His eyes never left mine, and I swear to God, I was on the verge of having a heart attack. He had to be able to feel my heart trying to beat out of my chest. I mean…his hand was *right there* and everything, so he surely had to feel it, right? Hell, he could probably *hear* it. I couldn't hear anything, except the blood rushing through my ears. And because I was a rookie, and because I didn't know what the hell was going on, my chest started to heave in huge breaths that just gave him more permission to touch me.

My voice was all gargled glass. "Damien, wh…what are y…you doing?"

He moved until his stomach was pressed up against my chest, and running the hand on my breast upward, he gripped the back of my neck and kissed me. He took his other hand and grabbed my hip and held me firm as his mouth did unexpected things to me. I could feel myself being swept away in the tornado that was Damien Greystone when I finally came to my senses.

I pulled my head back and pushed at his body. "No. Stop it, Damien."

He gave me a smirk in response. "Oh, really? Stop it? And why would I want to stop?"

I wanted to stab myself with a fork at my next words, but I couldn't help it. "Y...you can't come to me after being with He…Heather." I lifted my chin. "I'm better than that, even if you don't think I am." It disappointed me when my voice cracked. "There's a guy out there for me who will think so, too."

His eyes lit like a fire, and he clenched his jaw. "I'm not going to explain Heather or any other girl to you because you wouldn't believe me anyway. All you need to know is that I haven't been with her in the way you think I have." He put his hand back behind my neck again and his voice was all male and rust. "Also, there will never be another guy for you, Halloween. *Never.*"

Damien leaned down, and this time, he took the kiss. It wasn't soft or sweet or gentle. He was all force and dangerous energy. My entire body was humming with the sensation of *him*. His other hand found its way back to my hip and his grip was punishing. It felt like he was kissing me to survive, and I was getting high off the thought.

He maneuvered me backwards until the back of my legs hit the edge of my bed. All at once, I was hit with the realization of what exactly we were doing. He was here for my virginity, and I was inexplicably handing it over to him. Was I really so twisted by all his years of torment that he really was what I craved now? He's been awful towards me for years, yet here I was, wanting to do anything he asked of me. I must have been sicker and more broken than I thought. Weak and pathetic, I wanted him to finally like me.

He pulled away, ending the kiss, and I watched in fascination as he yanked his shirt over his head, leaving his torso bare. God, he was stunning. How could this boy possibly want to be with *me?*

Damien wasn't shy in his undress. He didn't stop until he was completely naked in front of me, shoes, socks, and all. Before I could get a good look, his hands were already lifting the edge of my tank top up and I numbly let him pull it over my head and toss it on the floor next to his clothes.

I wanted to ask him if he liked what he saw, but the growl emitting from his throat was encouragement enough. His green eyes never wavered from my brown ones as he hooked his fingers on either side of my panties and dragged them down my legs. I wanted to be embarrassed. I should have been embarrassed. I should have been mortified. I've only kissed one boy…well, one and half…and here I was, letting Damien strip me naked to take whatever he wanted from me.

He leaned into me until I was forced to lie down on the bed and his huge body lowered with me, covering me completely. I couldn't get a handle on my out-of-control breathing and every time I inhaled, the tips of my breasts would rub against his chest.

I wasn't sure what to expect. I mean, I've read novels and seen movies, but I knew that was make-believe and not a realistic interpretation of actual sex. "I don't know what to do," I confessed. "I...I don't know what you want from me."

He leaned his head down and started kissing my neck, and the pure euphoria of the act had me out of my mind with pleasure. "I just want you, Fiona. *Just you.*"

The next thing I knew, he settled in between my legs with his penis rubbing up against my center. *Oh, my God, this was really happening.* Before I had a chance to change my mind, I felt a searing pain ripping me apart from the inside. I was on the verge of letting out a scream so loud that it would surely bring the house down and my parents running, but Damien had immediately covered my mouth with his hand.

I was expecting him to wait until the pain had subsided and I was used to his size, but he didn't. He started ramming into me with no regard for my pain or discomfort. It was agony, and it consumed my entire being. It wasn't until after a few minutes that the pain lessened and something else took its place.

Pleasure.

Pleasure started surfacing in all the nerves that ran along my body. I didn't know what was happening, and I couldn't ask for his opinion because Damien kept his hand over my mouth as he used his other arm to brace himself above me.

Damien pushed into me faster and harder, and with each thrust, I was taken higher and higher into a world that didn't exist outside of drugs. I felt heat start at the center of my core and shoot out like a starburst throughout my body. I screamed louder than I did when he had ripped me open.

I felt Damien strain and lock up above me, and he let out a cursed, *"Fuuuuck,"* before collapsing on top of me. After a few quiet seconds, he removed his hand from my mouth, and just like that, he lifted off my body and I watched stunned as he began to dress.

"What now?" I whispered, feeling overwhelmed and scared. We hadn't used a condom and the stickiness between my thighs felt like a death sentence.

He didn't bother with looking at me as he finished dressing. "Nothing." And then I knew. "You didn't really think I'd leave for Yale without one last 'fuck you', did you?" He was halfway out the window when he finished slicing me open. "Have a nice life, Halloween."

CHAPTER 5

There's family, and then there are relatives.

Fiona - (Ten Years Later) ~

There were moments in your life that you remembered forever. They were embedded into your memory and no amount of alcohol in the world could make you forget them. There were always drugs, but even they could only make you forget for a little while.

My entire childhood was made up of moments I'd like to forget, so I knew that of which I spoke. But this one, right here, I couldn't contain my rage if I tried.

Sitting across from my parents, I asked the questions that made no difference because the answers wouldn't change the situation. "How could you do this? How could you not seek help before it got to this point? What the hell, Dad?"

"You better watch how you speak to me, Fiona. I am still your father and-"

His face was red, and I couldn't believe he had the audacity to puff up. "You've got a hell of a lot of nerve, Dad. Growing up, you let me live close to poverty because placing bets took priority over putting food on the table and you're going to utter the words 'I'm still your father' at me?" I looked over at my mother. She was quietly crying, playing the perfect accomplice to my father's addiction. "Then you guys call me over, telling me you're on the verge of losing everything you guys own, dumping *your* problem in my lap, and you have to balls to try to get demanding with me?" I let out a humorless scoff. "You have got to be kidding me."

"Fiona, please…" my mother pleaded.

"Please what, Mother? What is it you expect me to do here?"

My words didn't register with my father because he kept on like he was entitled to saving. "We are still your parents and deserve some respect, Fiona. You may not have had designer clothes and handbags growing up, but you did have clothes, not to mention food and a home."

This man was unbelievable. "Jesus Christ, Dad. I'm your daughter. All those things are basic things you were supposed to provide for me by law if not by conscience. If supporting me was such a burden, maybe you and Mom shouldn't have had kids. There's an idea."

"Fiona! Of course, that is not what your dad is implying. We love you, and of course, we wanted you." Mom darted a side glance towards my dad. "Your dad is just trying to remind you that family helps family, that's all."

"Family helps family?" I picked up all the documents that scattered the coffee table in their living room and waved them in the air. "These...*this*...this is not family asking family for help. Asking family for help is asking them to co-sign for a car loan or asking to crash on their couch until they get back on their feet. Family asking family for help is *not* asking them to come up with hundreds of thousands of dollars to cover their gambling debts because they're about to lose everything."

"Yes, it is," she argued. "When we both know that all you have to do is take a second mortgage out on your house or take out a loan against Fiona's."

I wish I could say I was surprised, but what life has taught me in my twenty-eight years was that, while people may love you, they don't necessarily love you in the way you would like for them to. My father had always been a reserved parent when I was growing up. He had spent most of his time working and fighting with my mom about all the things we couldn't afford. I sometimes wondered if his mistreatment of my mother had led me to crave the same kind of mistreatment from a certain boy at school growing up.

My mom did her best, but she was weak. She let herself believe that as long as we had food, clothes, and a home to live in that my dad's little problem wasn't really a problem. She did her best to shelter me from their arguments, but the older I got, the harder it had been to shield me.

Although I spent all my high school years studying my ass off, I hadn't graduated with straight A's. However, I had graduated with good enough grades to apply for and get partial scholarships. I was only forced to take out one loan that I had paid off as soon as I could. While it took most people four years to finish college, I had gone to community college, and because the day only has twenty-four hours in it, it had taken me six years to finish my BA in business management. I still planned on going back for my masters one day, though.

I had also started working at All Things Alice, a small coffee shop that sold baked pastries, while I was in college. The claim to Alice's fame had been that every pastry she sold had been a homemade hand-me-down family recipe. And each item she sold was delicious. She also had a small one-bedroom apartment over the shop that she had let me live in rent-free while I'd gone to school. If I owed anyone, I owed her. Everything she's ever done for me had been to help me be a better me, not to cash in on whatever I'd achieved.

I looked my dad in the same brown eyes that mirrored mine. "Are you seriously asking me to risk my home and my business to pay off your gambling debts?"

The man had no shame, but then most people with addictions didn't. "We're asking our daughter to help us out in our time of need."

I looked back at my mom. "Growing up, I suffered through our financial struggles just like you did, and I didn't ask you guys for anything when I chose to go to college. I worked, and I studied, and I created a life for myself with *no* help from you. Are you telling me, *as my mother*, I'm obligated as your daughter to risk it all for *him?*"

She broke down in sobs. "We'll lose everything, Fiona."

Well...I guess she's telling me exactly that.

I should probably feel some sort of sympathy for her, but I just couldn't help it. I was done being a doormat the night of my high school graduation. "Even if I did mortgage my house to the hilt and get a loan against Fiona's, it's not enough to cover the total amount of your debts. So even on the off chance that whoever holds your loans would work with us, how do you plan on paying off whatever's left?"

She darted a look at my dad, and that's when I knew what she's going to say next. "Well, Fiona's is very successful. We were thinking that you could arrange a payment plan or something. You can afford it, honey." She shook her head. "We simply can't."

I barked out a humorless laugh. "There are no words to describe just how callous and selfish you two are." I found I was more upset with my mother than I was with my father. "You are willing to stand by and watch your daughter lose everything she's ever worked hard for in order to save a man who doesn't give a shit about anything other than his next bet."

"That's enough Fiona!" my father finally interjected.

"Oh, on that we agree." I stood up to leave. I was not going to bail out my ungrateful, self-absorbed parents. "You guys are going to have to find your own way out of this mess. I'm not risking everything I have worked my entire life for because you have a problem you refuse to get help for."

My mother stood up with me. "What if he agrees to get help?"

At that, my father stood up absolutely incensed. "Maryanne, I do not need help. I enjoy betting every now and again, and that's it. It's not my fault if the bets fall bad."

"Do you hear yourself?" I shrieked. "You owe hundreds of thousands of dollars in gambling debt and you're seriously standing here telling us that you don't have a problem. You are on the verge of losing everything and you're still in denial? You are a real piece of work, Dad."

"Fiona, that's enough! This situation is hard enough without you pointing fingers and assigning blame," my mother snapped. "It doesn't matter how or why we got here, all that matters is that this is where we are, and we need your help." It seemed like my mom only had balls when it came to her daughter, but not when it came to Jared Eldstead.

"Mom, I am not going to bail you guys out just so he can continue with his not-a-problem gambling problem. If you end up homeless, you are more than welcome to live with me until you guys get back on your feet. However, I am not jeopardizing my home and business for you guys, and quite frankly, you guys are shitty parents for asking me to."

I didn't see the slap coming.

It took a few seconds for the pain to radiate across my cheek and into my eyes. Once it did, I cupped my cheek and applied pressure, hoping it would ease the burn shooting across my face.

"Jared!" I could hear my mother shout in disbelief.

"If you think I'm going to stand by and let you insult us-*your parents*-in our own home, you are mistaken young woman!"

If you were to ask me what I was feeling in this moment, I wouldn't be able to come up with one word in the English language. My father has never struck me before, so it should have given me an indication as to how desperate he really was, but all it did was make me loathe him more.

I turned, and without a word, I walked out of their house. If there was any chance of me helping them before, it was gone the instant his hand connected with my face.

What a bastard.

I got into my car and slammed the door shut once I was inside. I started up the car, but I sat there trying to breathe away my rage. My phone rang in my purse as I tried to calm down, and glancing down, I saw Vicky's name flashing across the screen. God, this crazy lady had perfect timing. I didn't know what I'd do without her.

"How may I help the crazies?" I answered.

"Personalized straitjackets would be a good start. I'm tired of the residents stealing mine all the time. How hard is it to sew on a name patch anyway?" Vicky replied.

I didn't expect any other kind of answer. It felt good to laugh. "What's up, chick?"

"Tell me you know I had a shitty day, so you went out and had a shitty day because you're loyal like that, and now we can both go to Mercury's and drink our shitty days away." I could hear her letting out a deep breath.

"What a coincidence. I was certain that you knew *I* was having a shitty day, so like the loyal friend *you* are, you went out and had a shitty day also, and you were going to offer to get an Uber, so we could get stupid drunk at Mercury's."

"Stupid drunk?" she asked. "Wow. I was just looking for a couple of drinks. We still have to be responsible adults in the morning, Fee. We need to limit stupid to Friday and Saturday nights, chickee."

"Fine, I'll reserve stupid for tomorrow, but I can meet you at Mercury's in about twenty minutes."

"See you there."

I hung up and pulled my car away from the curb. I made the ten-minute drive from my parents' house to my house that sat pretty much on the other side of town. Plus, it was closer to Fiona's, which made life that much more convenient.

Fiona's was what used to be All Things Alice. After I had finally graduated, Alice had asked me to stay on to-what she claimed was a favor at the time-help her go over all her financials and get her prepared for retirement. So, Alice had let me stay in the apartment for the next two years-rent-free again-as we had prepared for her retirement. Once she was all set, she had announced that she was selling All Things Alice and she really hoped I would be interested in buying it.

I had been shocked to say the least. And scared. This wonderful woman had wanted me to take over her life's work, and she'd had faith in me that I could.

That was a lot of pressure on a person.

When I had finally agreed, Fiona's First Cup had been born. I hadn't wanted to change the name, but Alice would have none of it. She had wanted me to have my own success, and she's the one who had actually come up with the new café name.

I was intimidated at first when we had started phasing out Alice's pastries. I had been sure the business would go under without her signature deserts, but surprisingly enough, it hadn't, and I had been able to convince Alice to come out of retirement once a month. So, the first Sunday of every month, Alice dropped off an array of her pastries and the stampede would begin.

I've been the owner of Fiona's for two years now, and while it may not be a huge world-changing successful business, it was my business, and it has done very well for me.

Now, if Alice asked me to mortgage everything that I owned to help her out, I would. That woman has been more of a parent to me in the ten years that I've known her than my own have been all my life. There was nothing I wouldn't do for Alice because there isn't anything she hasn't done for me.

It was a sad realization to know there was a difference between family and relatives. Alice and Vicky were my family-*my real family.*

One boring Uber car ride later, I was sitting at Mercury's waiting on Vee. I was halfway through my beer when I saw a flurry of red making its way towards me.

Vicky plopped down on the barstool next to mine as she dropped her purse on the bar. "I know a guy who can get us new identities within the next twenty-four hours. Let's kidnap Alice and leave this town and everyone in it." She threw her hand up to wave down the bartender, Hector.

I waited for her to place her order. "Do I get to pick my new name?"

She scoffed. "Of course. I'm not going to let him saddle us with names like Gertrude or Willomina. We'll pick sexy names like Chloe or Jessica. Alice can be Veronica."

"I like." I took a drink of my beer. "Okay, rock, paper, scissors for who goes first."

I won.

After ordering another beer, I went on to tell her everything that had happened at my parents from the second I walked into their house to the second I walked out and took her call in my car. Her face conveyed her utter shock. "Holy fuck balls, Fee."

"I know." I could only nod at her fuck balls assessment. "So, what about you?"

She shook her head. "After hearing all that, I just realized I've had a fantastic day. What are you going to do?"

I shrugged my shoulder. "I love my parents, but they're on their own."

CHAPTER 6

Call me a bastard, but I'm a bastard with a plan.

Damien ~

I stood in my new office looking out over the view that was San Francisco. It felt weird being back on the West Coast permanently. Or maybe it's because there was nothing left holding me back from finally being able to finalize my life's plan.

Come Monday, G&C Industries, Inc. will be an official coast-to-coast financial powerhouse. While it had taken a lot of hard work to get us to where we were, it hadn't been as hard as it could have been. Between Will's and my Yale educations and family names, a lot of doors had been opened to us. And once I'd gone after my father and had destroyed everything he built, let's just say my reputation as a man who didn't give fuck paved a lot of the rest of the way.

The door to my new office opened, and I turned to the voice of probably the only real friend I had in the world. "Hey, Dame, I see the design company did well in here, too."

I looked around, but I didn't see what Will saw. The room looked like an office. It was decorated in dark woods and brown fabrics. The only floor-to-ceiling glass window in the room faced the back of my desk which was part of the matching set of bookshelves, end tables, and small conference table that took up the left side of the office. Two matching armchairs sat directly in front of my desk and there was a freestanding bar in the right corner of the room. There was a door that led to a private restroom that I actually had designed into a small resting area. It contained a king-sized bed, a closet full of business attire, and a small standing shower alongside a toilet and sink area. I often worked around the clock, so I needed a place I could take power naps, if need be.

The artwork adorning the walls meant nothing to me. Oh, I was sure they were expensive and tasteful, but I didn't really give a fuck. There was only one personal item of mine in this entire room, and it was a framed picture of a brown-haired, brown-eyed obsession that sat on top of my desk.

"It's an office, Will. As long as I can work in here that's all I give a damn about."

Being my friend for as long as he has been, he wasn't put off by my remark. He plopped himself down on one of the armchairs and looked up at me. "So, you're really going to do this, huh?"

I simply nodded. He already knew the answer, so he really didn't need confirmation. Maybe he was still hoping he could talk me out of it.

William Creston has been my best friend since we were ten-years-old. If there was anyone on the planet who knew me well, it was him. He was also very aware of my sick, unreasonable obsession with a particular brunette.

When we were sixteen, I found Dennis Franks kissing my Fiona at a party. I'll never forget the blinding rage that had burned me from the inside out at the sight of another guy's lips and hands on her body. I had ripped him off of her, and had it not been for Will and Jake, I have no doubt I would have beaten Dennis to death.

The next day Will had made a comment along the lines of what did I care if Dennis popped Fiona's cherry and I had beaten *him* just as badly. Will had missed school for a week because of it. My parents had more money than a small country at the time, so I was sure his family was going to sue me for damages or make my parents buy my way out of jail, but Will had told his parents that he'd been riding drunk on an ATV and that's how he had ended up bruised and broken. I wasn't sure if anyone believed him, but without anyone else to dispute his story, they had to let it drop.

His first day back to school, I had jammed him up before football practice and had asked him why did he lie for me. He said he knew I had a thing for Fiona, he just never knew to what extent. Also, that I was his friend, so he was going to help me get over my obsession with her. From that day on, Will had rarely left my side, and he always made sure we'd been surrounded by girls. He had spent a lot of years trying to help me overcome my compulsions, but around the time we were in our third year of college, he realized his efforts had been all for naught. Nothing would cure me of my need for Fiona. *Nothing.* There was only ever that girl.

I knew what I'd done to her on graduation night had ruined her, but I couldn't help myself. There was no way I was going to go off to college and leave some other sonofabitch to take her virginity. That was mine. *She* was mine. What she hadn't known was that she hadn't been the only virgin in her bed that night. I had played around with other girls, but I had never fucked one. My first time had been hers. Everything else in my life had been hers, so that had been no different. Hell, I had been so out of my mind with my need for her that I hadn't even put on the condom I had brought with me. I had always known how it was going to go down, but I still had planned to protect her. When I found out she hadn't gotten pregnant from our encounter, I had been a little disappointed that I hadn't had an excuse to stay in touch with her.

It wasn't until my sophomore year in college that I had finally started fucking around with other girls. In a perfect world a person saves themselves for their one true love and there's never anyone else.

Well, my world wasn't and isn't perfect.

I didn't fuck at random though, and any girl I was with had either been a blonde, redhead, or very light-haired brunette and skinny-*no curves*. I never fucked a girl who had dark brown hair or dark brown eyes. I guess it was my fucked-up way of being half-ass faithful in my obsession with Fiona. And I have never fucked a female without a condom save for that one and only time with her.

My life's plan had always been to come back for her. Will knew this, even if he thought that it was a bad idea. That's how we came about having an East Coast home office and now a West Coast home office. Will and I were equal partners, and he was going to be in charge of G&C East, and I was going to oversee G&C West.

I perched myself on the edge of my desk and crossed my arms over my chest. "I'm taking tomorrow off and heading down to Smithtown in the morning." Luckily for me, Smithtown was only an hour's drive southeast of San Francisco.

"I wouldn't be your best friend if I didn't at least try to talk you out of this one last time, Dame."

I smirked. "I wouldn't expect anything less."

"I know it's been ten years, Dame, but there's a very realistic chance she still hates you."

"It doesn't matter if she still hates me or not. She doesn't get a choice in this, Will. She never did."

He stood up and walked over to the bar to pour himself a drink. I didn't blame him. I couldn't imagine how hard it was to know that your best friend and partner in business was fucking crazy. "Just do me a favor, okay? Before it gets to the point where you're going to commit kidnapping and false imprisonment, call me first. Give me one last chance to save you and everything we've built. You know, as a courtesy."

My laugh wasn't humorous at all, mostly because if things didn't go as planned, kidnapping and false imprisonment weren't necessarily off the table. "Fine. I promise to call before I flee the country with her."

Will grimaced. "Jesus, I wish I didn't know you were serious."

It all started the first day of kindergarten. Fiona had walked into Miss Julie's class and one look at her had me feeling things I couldn't comprehend at the young age of five. There were a lot of feelings I didn't understand at that age, and up until I had laid eyes on Fiona, the feelings I had been mostly acquainted with were anger, sadness, and helplessness.

See, I had lived in a dollhouse growing up; a very rich, elegant, fake, perfectly imposturous dollhouse. If there was ever a candlestick out of place or a dinner not cooked to perfection, there'd been hell to pay, usually in the form of my father smacking my mother around. I couldn't even begin to explain what it does to a young male mind to grow up watching your father beat on your mother. You're supposed to be growing up to become a man, but your only example of that was anything but.

When I first saw Fiona walk into Miss Julie's class with her shiny brown hair in identical curly ponytails and dressed in a pink shirt under blue overalls rolled up at the legs, I remember feeling like I had been suffocating.

I had watched her run around making new friends and when I had first heard her laugh, I just remember feeling such anger at her happiness. Sure, the other kids in class had laughed and played, but none of them had sounded like she had. None of them *glowed* like she had.

The day she approached me offering to color with me had been my undoing. I had avoided being close to her because she had made me feel strange, but when she stood in front of me that day and I had looked into those hypnotizing chocolate orbs or hers, I had never felt so scared. She had made me feel like I was big enough and strong enough to run home and protect my mother from my father. She had made me feel powerful and frightening. She had made me feel like all the scary, bad guys in movies; guys who killed anyone who got in their way. She had made me want to drag her behind me and let no one near her. *Ever.* Fiona had made me feel like the protector I knew I couldn't be at only five-years-old.

As the years went by, I had perfected the art of being Damien Sebastian Greystone III, perfect son to Grace and Damien Greystone II, straight-A student, and star athlete. The only variable in my life had been Fiona. She'd been the only thing on the planet that made me feel or do things that weren't part of the role that had been my life. She had made me feel…well, everything.

I had felt envy at her contentment with having just one friend. I had felt disgusted that she had been forced to wear secondhand clothes when she should have been draped in silks and satins. I had felt shame every time she cowered at my bullying instead of rising in bravery. I had felt anger every time she gifted some asshole with one of her signature smiles. And I had felt *unbridled rage* every time a guy mentioned her name.

However, as we got older, lust, lust was what I had felt the most when I would look at her. When we had reached our puberty years, it was a wonder I hadn't end up in juvenile hall for all the things I almost did. Fiona' s body had started filling out and being cruel to her had been the only way I knew of to keep myself from hauling her off and just *taking* her. She had grown into an hourglass figure and every goddamn day it seemed as if her hair got shinier, her eyes got brighter, her skin got softer, and her body got hotter.

I lost count of how many faces I busted before kids at school had finally got the message to not mention Fiona around me. I spent a better part of my high school years dancing back and forth between rage, lust, and possessiveness.

It's a wonder I hadn't lost my fucking mind.

Ten years later, I was back to finally make her mine. A small part of me had hoped that, once I had left for college and she was no longer in my face every day, that I'd move on from her, but I hadn't. If anything, being away from her had just driven me crazier. The need to get back to her had been what had driven me to work around the clock and get G&C to need a West Coast home base, and now that I was here, nothing was going to stop me from having Fiona.

I took pity on Will. "It's going to be fine, Will. I'm pretty certain she still hates me, but I've got a plan for that."

The corner of his lip lifted in disbelief. "Yeah, I just bet you do. I'm sure it's foolproof, too."

I reached for the glass of…well, I had no idea what he had poured for me. "Have you ever considered that she may have feelings for me, as well?" I took a drink. Ahhh, whiskey.

"I'm sure she feels all kinds of things for you, Dame. Rage, disgust, regret, anger, rage…"

"You mentioned rage twice," I pointed out.

"It needs to be mentioned twice. You tormented that girl for thirteen years, Dame. Count them…*thirteen*."

"Yes, I did," I agreed. "I'll be the first to admit I was horrible to her. Still, why would a girl who I bullied and hurt for thirteen years give me her virginity? She kissed me back that night I fucked Dennis up, and she let me climb into her bedroom window the night of graduation and gave herself to me. Why would she do that if she didn't feel *something* for me, Will?"

And here came the reason that we've stayed friends for so long. "Oh, I don't know, maybe because she was a young, dumb, and horny teenager and you were available?" he suggested. "Young teenage boys do not have the market cornered on horniness. If we did, all girls would be virgins until their wedding night." Will down the last of his drink before saying, "Don't kid yourself into thinking that just because she didn't have any boyfriends that she didn't have any desires that she needed to be fulfilled."

My stomach lurched at his words. In my world, she had been with me because she had feelings for me. I wouldn't have it any other way. "Be that as it may, it was still *me* who had to wash her blood off my dick when I got home that night. I don't care what her reasoning was back then. She still let me be her first."

"Jesus Christ, Damien. I didn't need that visual."

"And I don't need you trying to steer me down another path." I finished my drink and placed the empty glass on my desk. "Everything I've done and everything I am right now has always led up to her. That's why G&C is set up as unconventional as it is. If I crash and burn, you'll still be protected financially," I reminded him.

Will narrowed his eyes at me. "I give two fucks about the money,

Greystone. I've always had it and I know how to always make it. If I ever find myself on the street eating out of a paper bag, so be it. What I care about is your fucking sanity. You're my best friend, dude. If this doesn't work out, I fear for your *sanity,* not our fucking money."

I'd hug him, but I wasn't a little bitch. "Duly noted."

I could see his chest rise and fall with the last of his advice. "Alright, I'm going to head back to New York and let you get on with your plan of pillaging and beheading."

"Thanks, I appreciate it."

He walked his way towards the door. "I'm only a call and a couple of thousands of miles away." I just nodded because I knew he was serious.

After he shut the door behind him, I walked around my desk and sat down on the ridiculously expensive leather desk chair. I reached across the office phone and picked up the framed picture of Fiona I had sitting on my desk.

It was one of the many pictures the PI I had on her had taken over the years. It was a picture of her working behind the counter the first day Fiona's First Cup opened. It was a picture of the woman who held my entire life in her hands, and she didn't even know it.

CHAPTER 7

The devil never really ever leaves you alone.

Fiona ~

The day was almost over, thank God. Normally, I loved coming to work and doing what I did, but yesterday's disaster with my parents still had me in a funk. Lost count of how many beers and a couple tequila shots later had done nothing to erase the incident from my mind.

I also hadn't slept for shit because, even after all my tough talk yesterday, I still stayed up half the night trying to work a way to help them out that didn't involve sacrificing my home or business.

My father had a problem and the little girl in me wanted to believe that just maybe-*maybe*-if I helped them out, he would go to counseling and finally become the dad I always dreamed of. Then they'd finally be happy and that would allow them to finally be happy for me.

I was such a fucking idiot.

Seriously. I should have a medal in idiotism or something.

I was going over some bank statements when my assistant manager, Debbie, cracked open my office door. "Hey, there's a guy out here who says he needs to speak with you."

"Is he here for a job?"

She shook her head. "Nah, he said something about settling a debt with you?" Her face took on a look of confusion, and she just shrugged one of her dainty shoulders.

My face must have mirrored hers because I didn't have-

Shit. Shit. Shit. My goddamn parents.

"Oh…uh, go ahead and send him back. I'm sure he's just confused. I'll take care of it."

When Debbie left to go get him, I stood up and rounded my desk. I'd never felt so anxious before in my life and that was saying something. I just had a gut feeling that I did not want to be sitting down looking up at the guy when he walked in. He had obviously been told by my parents that I would handle their debt, so I needed to stand strong and come across firm when I corrected him.

There was a light, respectful knock on the door before Debbie opened it. "Come in."

I smiled at Debbie as she walked in first and held the door open for...*Damien Greystone?*

Holy Mary, Jesus, and Joseph.

Walking in the room like he owned it was Damien fucking Greystone, and all I could do was stand here and die of the heart attack I was so clearly having.

Debbie immediately closed the door after Damien cleared the path, and if she found it odd that I hadn't greeted him, she didn't say anything before walking out.

Damien Greystone was standing in my office and oh, Sweet Baby Jesus, he was gorgeous. He'd always been beautiful as a kid and then a teenage boy. But standing before me as a man, Damien was breathtaking. His hair was still dark as evil, and while it was cut short on the sides, the top length of it fell around his head like his hair didn't give a fuck, either. His dark black brows arched perfectly over those deep green lasers of his. His eyes looked greener if that was possible. His face grew into sharp slants and edges and was void of any hair, ready to slay any female with a pulse should he flash a smile that I knew came with a deep set of crescent-shaped dimples.

He was dressed in a suit that I knew cost more than my daily profits. I knew this because it draped his body with tailored perfection. He looked taller, bigger, and more imposing. And he was looking at me like he wanted to chew me up and spit me out like the insect under his shoe that I was.

I decided to put my heart attack on hold to ask him what the hell was going on. "What are you doing here, Damien?"

He tilted his head slightly to the right as if he were puzzled, but I knew better. This man was never puzzled by anything. He always knew what cards everyone at the table were holding. "I thought your friend out there had explained. I'm here to settle your parents' debt."

I walked back around my office to place the desk in between us. I knew it looked cowardly, but I needed to put some space between us. I folded my arms across my chest. "*Exactly*. My *parents'* debt, not mine."

I was in such shock at seeing him, I didn't notice the folder in his hand until he flung it on top of my desk. "Your father's gambling debt to be specific."

I didn't reach for the folder. "That still isn't my debt."

I had so many questions, the first being how in the hell did he become the holder to all my father's debts. How was that even possible? For ten years, I tried to erase this man from my memories, and the entire time he's been exchanging money and shaking hands with my father? Damien *hated* me. Why would he have anything to do with my family if he didn't have to?

Luckily for me, Damien wasn't one to dick around, and he was more than happy to crumble my world around me. "You're right. It's not your debt and you are technically not obligated to pay it. However, if you don't want to see either of your parents in jail, you will."

I guess I could add passing out to having a heart attack because if I didn't sit down, I was pretty sure I might faint. "Jail?"

He sat down on the chair across from my desk as I sat down in my chair. He jutted his chin towards the folder he put on my desk. "Everything I need to put both your parents in jail for a long time is in that folder there. Copies, of course, but still."

My gaze didn't waver, and I didn't open the folder. "Why don't you explain it to me, Damien?"

His lip curled just a bit, but he complied. "About five years ago I bought out Smithtown Textiles. I'm sure I don't have to tell you that your father is one of the office administrators there. However, I'm not sure if you know that he was promoted to the accounting department about three years ago, where he immediately began embezzling from the company."

No. Oh, God, no.

"It was suspected a little over a year ago and a full investigation was launched." He crossed his left ankle over his right knee and grabbed his leg as he rested his arm over his body. "The amounts started out fairly small and unnoticeable, but during this past year they've increased incredibly."

My hands trembled as I opened to folder. There were account statements, canceled checks, and pictures of my father entering and exiting gambling facilities. As I continued to flip through the papers, I found loans against their house, promissory notes, and even a picture of my father in a strip club all over a naked redhead.

Oh, God, I was going to throw up; throw up in front of Damien Greystone.

"Shall I continue?" he taunted.

I looked back up at him. "By all means, please do." I was happy my voice sounded steady.

"I'll save you the trouble of looking for it, but the total amount equals to a little over four-hundred grand, Halloween,"

I couldn't help the ferociousness that left my lips. "*Don't* call me that." The gorgeous sonofabitch just arched a brow and lifted the corner of his mouth in a smirk.

Point one for him.

"Then I'll cut right to the chase, *Fiona.*" Damien set his left foot back on the floor, then leaning over, he placed his elbows on his knees and clasped his hands before him. "If the debt is not settled, your parents are going to prison for a long time. Your father for embezzlement and your mother for being an accomplice and using those monies to finance her lifestyle."

I jumped out of my seat so quickly that my chair nearly fell over.

"Lifestyle? *What* lifestyle? You're talking like she's walking around town draped in diamonds and furs."

He leaned back in the chair but kept his eyes on me. "I don't care if she's walking around in a dirty, used, secondhand jacket. That jacket was purchased with money that didn't rightfully belong to her, and since she's never worked, it can't be argued that she bought anything with her own money."

I was shaking with rage and helpless frustration. "You are such a bastard."

"I never claimed to be otherwise, baby."

I wasn't violent by any means, but the fury coursing through my body had me wanting to murder this man with my bare hands. "You have everything they own already signed over to you…I ca…can sign over my house as well. That should cover most of it."

"Yes, I suppose. However, the profit on your homes all depends on their market value and what is still owned on the original loans, am I right?"

He knew he was right, the fucking prick. "You want Fiona's, don't you? That's what this is about, isn't it?"

He stood up and walked over towards me until he was invading my personal space, and he did it on purpose. I wasn't a stranger to his bullying tactics. Yeah, it's been ten years, but the last ten years hadn't done enough to erase the thirteen before then.

I didn't flinch and I didn't step back. I wasn't a ten-year-old girl anymore, protecting her new art bag. I was a grown ass woman who was protecting her home, her business, and her livelihood.

And now her parents' freedom, apparently.

Damien reached out and twirled a loose strand of my hair around his finger and I immediately felt the bottom of my stomach fall out. The last time I was with this man, he had left me bleeding all over my bed sheets, and now it seemed like he was back for more blood.

"Don't touch me," I hissed.

"Get used to it, Halloween, because I'm going to be touching you a lot in the near future."

I fixed my brown eyes onto his green ones. "Wh...what are you talking about?"

He hadn't let go of my hair when he answered, "I've got a proposition for you."

Every hair on my body stood at attention, his words as smooth as silk. "No."

He began to crowd me until the back of my thighs hit my desk. "Eager to see your parents in prison, are you? I mean, I know your father's a dick, but I thought you still loved your mother, at least."

"I'll sign over my house and my business," I conceded, and I didn't even bother trying to hide the moisture pooling in my eyes. I'd like to think I would have stood stronger had I not been blindsided by Damien coming back into my life. However, I knew that no matter who had held the debt, I couldn't stomach my mother going to prison all because she was stupidly in love with my father.

"You can," he agreed, "but I already have a house and a business. I don't need another of each."

I wanted to scream, cry, and kick this asshole in his nut sack. "Then what do you want, Damien? Quit playing fucking games with me and tell me what all this is all about."

"What it's always been about, Halloween. *You.*"

I shook my head. He couldn't mean…? *No way.* There was just no fucking way.

I guess he could see the dawning in my eyes because he smirked again and confirmed my suspicions. "I want you in exchange for dropping the charges and clearing your parents of all debt and criminal accusations."

No, no, no. He couldn't be serious. He...he just *couldn't.*

I wasn't sure how I was able to hold his gaze, I was just happy that I could. "What does that mean, exactly?"

"It means that if you accept my proposition, then you're mine for the next six months."

"Yours for six months," I numbly repeated.

Damien nodded. "You'll be my…uh…somewhat of a *girlfriend* for the next six months."

I knew my eyes were the size of saucers. "Oh, God…" My knees gave out on me and I would have gone crashing to the floor if he hadn't wrapped his arms around me to hold me up.

This time, I really was having a heart attack. All my insides suddenly felt too large for my body and it felt like they were bursting to escape.

This man hated me in an extremely singular way. He didn't want me to play the part of his girlfriend. Men usually treated their girlfriends with adoration and respect. Damien Greystone did not adore or respect me. So, that meant he could only want one thing from me. Apparently, he hadn't been done with me on graduation night after all.

Growing up, he had turned me into a weakling, a coward, a scared mouse, and now that we were all grown up, it looked like he wanted to turn me into a whore.

His whore.

For six months.

I felt like I was five-years-old all over again, feeling the punch of his rejection at not wanting to be my friend. The pools in my eyes finally spilled over. "Why?"

The phone on my desk rang, saving him from having to answer. He stopped playing with my hair and took a decent-sized step back from me. "How about I let you get back to work and give you a few hours to think about it."

He really was a bastard. He knew there wasn't much to think about. Either

I fucked him on command, or my parents would be sent to rot in prison.

I stood silently as I watched him head for the door. "I'm staying at The Embassy, room 500. I'll expect you at exactly six o'clock. If you're even a second late, your parents will be getting arrested at precisely six-ten. We clear?"

I nodded like a simpleton and I stayed silent as he shut the door behind him.

I ignored the ringing phone. If it was important, whoever was calling will leave a message. I looked at the clock on the wall and saw that it was already a little past four.

Hours to think about it, my ass.

Not that there was a whole lot to think about. I couldn't let my parents go to prison. I wished I could let them. I wanted to be able to walk away from this and let them reap what they sewed, but Damien was offering a way to save my parents without losing everything I worked so hard for.

I'd just have to push my dignity and self-respect aside for six months.

CHAPTER 8

Being a functioning psychopath was a real thing.

Damien ~

I couldn't lie; I spent the last two hours since I left Fiona feeling like my skin was trying to crawl off my body. I'd like to say I wasn't a big enough bastard to send her parents to jail, but I was. If I was going to spend the rest of my life drowning in misery, then so the fuck was she.

It had taken strength I hadn't even known I possessed to keep from flipping up the skirt she'd been wearing earlier and just taking her on top of her desk. Her beauty had always rendered me stupid, but Fiona as a grown woman was proof that God and Satan existed. Fiona had a face created by God and a body created by Satan. Add that to her personality and...well, it made her walking, talking, breathing sin and salvation all at the same time.

I'd never felt such relief in my life as I had the second that I heard the knock on the suite door. I opened the door to find a very pissed off Fiona on the other side. I stepped back to give her enough room to walk in. I didn't say anything as she surveyed the room. It was a nice room as far as suites went, but at the end of all this, all I cared about was that it had a bed big enough for me to fuck her on in every position I've ever imagined.

I was too eager to care about subtlety. "So, you got an answer for me, Halloween?"

Her posture snapped, and she slowly turned around to face me. She wasn't the timid girl from school anymore, I'd give her that. "Is 'fuck you' a good enough answer?"

I laughed at her defiance. "Yes, it is." I walked over to one of the end tables that decorated the sitting area and picked up my phone. She eyed me as I dialed the PI that I had on retainer for everything Fiona. "Yeah, Andrews? This is Greystone."

"What's up, man?" He had answered on the first ring. Smart man.

"Can you take what you have on the Eldsteads-"

"Damien, please don't," she hastened.

Never moving my eyes from hers, I stopped. "Never mind, Andrews."

I hung up the phone. "So, does this mean you're ready to give me a different answer?"

She dropped her purse over the back of the couch and let it land on the cushions. She looked around the room again, probably wanting to put off uttering the words that would change her life for as long as possible.

I waited patiently until she finally faced me. "I ac…accept your agreement. I'll…uh…date you for six months if you let my parents off the hook."

What I really wanted to do was drag her by her hair to the Justice of the Peace, but I figured I should stick with the plan of baby steps. So, instead, I nodded. "At the end of the six months, I'll hand over everything I have on your parents. However, your father does not get off unscathed. He will have to attend gamblers anonymous in order to keep his job."

She shook her head sadly. "I've tried, Damien, but he won't-"

"He will," I insisted. "I'll take care of it, Fiona."

If I wasn't so sure of the hatred that she had for me, I would swear I saw gratitude in her deep russet eyes. My goal at the end of all this was to have her so madly in love with me that she'll be signing her name Fiona Greystone in six months. But I knew the odds were more in favor of her pleading 'not guilty' to involuntary manslaughter after she killed me in a haze of hate and rage. I was willing to risk it, though.

Starting now.

We both knew who held all the cards here, so since I didn't need to establish my dominance, I went to her. If I were a better man, I'd give her more time to get used to our arrangement. I'd take her to dinner and attempt to ease her discomfort. However, I wasn't a better man and I've waited ten years to have her again. I had every intention of keeping her on her back until the sun came up tomorrow.

"Are you on birth control?" No sense in dancing around the practicalities.

"Yes."

That was it. Just a simple 'yes', and nothing more.

"When was your last physical?"

I could see her bristle a little bit at the question. "Last year sometime."

I raised a brow at her stubbornness. She knew exactly what I was trying to get to. What she didn't know was that I already knew everything I needed to know about her. The PI I had was the best. I could even tell you when her period was due. That's how fucking sick I was over this woman. "Anything I need to know?"

"Nope."

I stepped into her personal space and grabbed her by her upper arm. "When was the last time you fucked someone?"

I could feel the intake of her breath. "That's none of your business."

"I have to disagree, Halloween."

She got right back up in my face. "When was the last time *you* fucked someone?"

"I've never fucked anyone without a condom and I'm healthy. That's all you need to know."

Her face flushed red, and I knew it was because she knew my statement wasn't entirely accurate. I *have* fucked once before without a condom. "You're a liar," she hissed.

The woman had balls enough to address the elephant in the room, I'd give her that. "My apologies. Please allow me to rephrase." I leaned down farther into her personal space. "I've never fucked anyone *besides you* without a condom."

Her chest heaved and another inch and her tits would be brushing up against my stomach. "Well, same here. I have no health issues and I make sure I learn from my mistakes, so I have always used a condom with my partners."

I was unreasonably seething inside at her comment of using protection with her partners. In the last ten years, my PI had reported her dating a guy named Grady Waterston when she was twenty, but that had only lasted a couple of months. My guess was it had been too hard to juggle work, college, and a boyfriend. He later reported her dating a guy named Eric Singleton shortly after she had graduated from college, but again, that had only lasted a couple of months. It had been around the time she had gotten onboard with helping Alice McEntire run her business. The latest report was that she had started casually dating a guy named Jason Marks. They started dating about six months ago, and while my PI hasn't ever caught them having any slumber parties, I knew good, old Jason wasn't still hanging around if she hadn't already laid down with him.

I could admit her number was far smaller than mine, and I didn't give a fuck how chauvinistic that made me, but the knowledge that another man knew how she sounded and what she looked like when she came had the psychopath in me ready to murder the entire town.

"Well, I think it goes without saying that during these next six months there won't be any other *partners* in on this."

She darted her eyes away from mine and began to bite her lower lip. I almost lost my mind at her hesitation. The beast in me was trying to claw his way out of my soul, and if she didn't fucking answer me soon, I was going to let him out.

She finally returned her attention towards me. "Okay…I…that sounds reasonable, and it's safer to be monogamous." She tried to laugh off the seriousness of my demand. "I mean, how hard can it be to remain monogamous for six months, right?"

I gave her a pass but only because she truly didn't have any idea how deep my obsession with her ran. I knew she believed all this was just a game of power and manipulation, and while it was, it was born out of my desperation to have her. If anyone asked me if I loved this woman, I would tell them no.

What I felt for Fiona went beyond common love. What I felt for her was an all-consuming state of madness. If she had any clue as to what she did to me, she'd flee the country posthaste.

But I would still find her.

"Good. You wouldn't want anything bad to happen to good, old Jason, now, would you?"

Her eyes rounded to the size of platters. "How do-"

"Doesn't matter what I know or how I know it. Just know that I have enough money to know everything I need to know about you, including who you're fucking." I shook her slightly with the grip I still had on her arm. "In the morning, you're going to give Jason a call and convince him that you've moved on." She opened her mouth to protest but I didn't let her speak. "Do not test me on this, Fiona. If that man comes anywhere near you while you belong to me, I will fucking *destroy* him and everything he has, then I'll go after Vicky and Alice." I shook her harder. "And then I'll go after *you*. Understood?"

Her beautiful brown eyes flooded in a teary rage. *"I hate you."*

"I don't care what you feel for me, Halloween, as long as I make you feel *something."* I slammed my lips down on hers and the feeling of euphoria washed over my body like the first waves of heroin hitting an addict's blood stream.

I ran my hand up the back of her neck and fisted a chunk of her chocolate masses so tightly that she let out a strained moan. I could only hope it was hurting her. This first time was all for me. It was to feed my obsession and give me a semblance of sanity. I had the rest of the night to take care of her later, but right now I needed this hit.

I pulled back on the kiss and stared down at her swollen lips. Her eyes were glassy and lidded. "Never forget, you *chose* this, Fiona. That means you will act like you want me, even if you don't. That means you don't ever get to say no to me. That means you are mine to dress, to feed, to wash, to kiss, and to fuck however I want. Tell me you understand the rules."

She was breathing so hard that I was afraid she might hyperventilate. Still, the look in her eyes wasn't exactly hate. "I un…understand, Damien."

"Good." That was all that needed to be said before my lips descended on hers again.

This time she opened her mouth and let me inside. I swept my tongue alongside hers and I wanted to pledge everything I owned to God when she started actively kissing me back. With my right hand still tangled up in her hair, I ran my left hand down her neck and chest until I held the weight of one of those heavy, delicious tits.

Ten years ago, I had been too young, too crazy, and too desperate to worship her like I should have. Tonight, my tongue would learn every inch of her body, my fingers would massage every entrance she had, my hands would memorize all her curves, and my dick would shower her entire body, inside and out, with my cum.

Fiona grabbed onto my waist and I could feel her curl her fingers into the leather of my belt. I took that as a sign that she was turned on, and so I started walking her backwards towards the bed.

On our journey to the bed, clothes were being ripped off and discarded like the nuisances there were. The more Fiona took part in the stripping, the more encouraged I became. She may hate me, but she didn't hate my touch, and I would take what I could get from her.

As soon as I felt the back of her thighs hit the bed, I worked at lightning speed to remove her bra and panties as they were the only things left on her body. I found the resolve to step away from her and I lost the power of speech as I took in a grownup, naked Fiona.

As soon as she realized that I was taking in every inch of her magnificent body, she curled into herself trying to hide her body from my view. I place my hands on her shoulders and pushed them back to make her stand taller…well, as tall as her five-foot-two-inches would allow. "Never hide from me, Halloween. I've been fantasizing about your body for more years than I can count." I decided to give her a little bit of real honesty. "Graduation night, I wanted you so badly that I didn't take the time to look and appreciate what you were giving me." Her eyes were bugging out of her head so comically that I almost laughed. "I won't be making that same mistake tonight. By the time I'm done with you, your entire body will be burned into my memory." I was going to own every fucking inch of her.

"Damien…" she whispered astonished.

"Baby, I'm going to worship every inch of you," I promised. "Get up on the bed and just lay back for me."

I was shocked as shit when she obeyed me argument-free. I stood transfixed as she scooted herself backwards until her head rested on the ridiculous number of pillows on the bed. They propped her body up giving me a direct view of her massive tits, so I really shouldn't bad mouth the abundance of pillows.

I dropped my boxers, and I knew there was no way she couldn't see how rock solid hard I was. Her eyes widen-God let that be with awe and not pity-and I quickly climbed up on the bed to cover her. Fiona instinctively opened her legs to accommodate me and the second that her body cradled my cock, I knew I would never want to be anywhere else but here for the rest of my life.

I held myself up with my elbows and just took my time looking down at her face. "God, you're so fucking beautiful." Her eyes glossed over, and call me a pussy, but I wanted to tell her how sorry I was for everything, how much I loved her, and have always loved her, and ask her to marry me all at once.

I should have known it wouldn't be that easy.

"Don't say things like that to me, Damien." She tilted her head back a little, strengthening her resolve. "I'm here for you to fuck and nothing more.

Don't act like you give a shit about me now."

I didn't blame her considering that all she knew about me was what I've shown her, but that knowledge did nothing to curb the animal she riled up with her words. "So, you just want a repeat of graduation night? You want me to just take from you, is that it?"

Then she cut me to ribbons. "I was never confused into thinking you would do anything *but* take from me. You've been doing it since we were five."

I was so pissed that she had every right to think that, so I decided to show her the bastard she believed me to be. "In that case, know that it's going to only be until *I'm* satisfied that I'll leave your body alone. Until then, I don't care how sore, bruised, or battered you are. I won't stop until I'm *done* with you."

CHAPTER 9

It's not only the professionally diagnosed that are crazy.

Fiona ~

I wasn't sure what prompted me to bait him, I just knew the gentleness he showed me was fucking with my head. I didn't want him telling me I was beautiful. I didn't want him caressing me tenderly. I wanted-no-I *needed* him to use me ruthlessly if I was going to make it out of this arrangement with any kind of sanity left to speak of. I didn't want to like him.

I tried to be realistic and practical, but it was pretty evident I was out of my mind crazy. I mean, what other explanation could there be for me actually *liking* the way he was kissing and touching me? The second I felt his lips on mine and his hands on my body, I had been a goner. I was a pathetic, sad, desperate, confused goner. How could his touch feel *so* good when I hated him so much?

I've only been touched by three other men after graduation night and none of what they had done to me came close to how inflamed Damien made my body feel. I was definitely going to need professional couch-time therapy after these next six months…three times a week, most likely.

Damien started at my right ear and started kissing his way down my neck and it felt sooooooo deliciously sinful. I wanted to cry because he wasn't doing anything special. My fucked-up mind knowing that it was *him* kissing me was what made it feel so good. I let out an involuntary moan there was no way I could keep in.

He kept moving his way down my body until he was in perfect position to take a nipple into his mouth, and when he did, my body almost skyrocketed off the bed. He took both my breasts in his hands and kneaded the flesh as he alternated between sucking, laving, and biting both harden tips.

"Oh, God…" I shamelessly ran my fingers through his hair and held him close as he tasted and teased me. "Damien…"

He stopped pleasuring my breasts and moved his way up my neck until his lips reached my ear again. "What's wrong, baby? Are you disappointed I'm not ramming my cock into your hot pussy yet?"

His dirty words were making me wetter than I have ever been, but I had to put up at least some kind of resistance, right? "I don't care what you do to me," I lied.

He stilled above me but continued to speak into my ear. "Is that right?" Next thing I knew, he had wrapped his hand in my hair, fisting a good chunk of it, and yanked my head back so hard that my eyes watered. He peered down at me and his green eyes had never looked so alive. "In that case, I will ignore every time the word 'no' comes out of your mouth, Halloween. If you *don't care*, then you won't mind when I'm fucking this smart mouth of yours so hard that you choke on it. If you *don't care*, then you won't mind when I slide my cock between these huge tits of yours and cum all over them. If you *don't care*, then you won't mind me fucking that hot little cunt of yours, even after it's so swollen from use that I have to force it to take my cock." He tugged harder on my hair and all it did was make me flood the sheets. He leaned down and finished his little speech in between bites to my lower lip. "If you *don't care*, then you won't mind when I paint your face, tits, pussy, and ass with my cum. If you *don't care*, Halloween, then you won't mind it when I bury my cock balls-deep in your ass, will you, baby?"

I let out a humiliating cry at how hot every word out of his mouth sounded. Jason was the only person I actually slept with after Damien and both times had been lukewarm at best.

God, I was sick.

He let go of my hair and went back to kissing his way down my body. There was so much I wanted to say. So much I wanted to rant and rave at, but I couldn't find the words that wouldn't make it sound like I've been crying over him all these years. My pride was taking a serious beating as it was with every time I moaned or relented to his machinations.

He worked his way down my body until his shoulders prevented my legs from being able to close. Damien Greystone was seconds away from going down on me and I couldn't wait.

I felt his big hands splay on the insides of my thighs and push out. I could feel his breath on my wet lips, and I wanted to scream out for him to get to it already. However, I was still trying to salvage any pride I could at the moment. I was trying to convince myself I didn't want this.

I lost all thoughts of pride and grudges the second I felt his tongue sweep through my wetness. *"Damien…"* My hands instantly tangled themselves in the waves of his black hair and my grip was so strained that I could feel my nails digging into my palms. His hands curled around my thighs and I knew his fingers were going to leave bruises in my flesh, but I did not give one fuck.

Count them...Not. One. Fuck.

That's how mind-numbing the pleasure I was feeling was.

Mind. Numbing.

"Fuck, baby, I could eat this sweet pussy forever." Right now, in this insane moment in time, forever sounded just fine to me.

Damien didn't let up once he got his first taste of me. All I felt was euphoria as his tongue licked up and down my slit, circling and pushing on my clit every time he swept upwards.

My body tensed when I felt his fingers begin to invade my pussy. Damien was well over six-foot, making him big and solid everywhere, including his fingers. I moaned as they deliciously stretched me open. I could *hear* the wetness he was coaxing out of my body.

He paused long enough to tell me his plans. "I'm not stopping until you cum all over my face and fingers, Halloween. And when you do, I'm going to lap up every last drop. I'm going to taste you on my tongue for days after, baby."

I lifted my hips at his words, silently begging for more. He took the hint and went back to sliding his fingers inside my hot core and his tongue began to focus on my sensitive nub.

Within seconds, I could feel the tightening in my core in warning. I was on the verge of doing exactly what he wanted and cumming all over his face and fingers. *"Damien…"*

I could feel myself clench around his fingers and that small action prompted him to curl his fingers deeper in and hit his target and it was enough. I wasn't sure if I came from his tongue on my clit or his fingers brushing up against that secret spot, but my nerves electrified in a blaze of unparalleled pleasure that my body shook with the force of it.

"*Jesus fucking Christ,*" I heard him growl through the haze of my orgasm.

My body was still twitching when I finally noticed Damien hovering over me. I could barely keep my eyes open, let alone focus. "Baby, look at me."

I blinked a few times and finally managed to focus on his green gaze. I brought my hand around and placed my palm on his cheek and just *looked* at him. The devil shouldn't be so beautiful. I should hate this man. I *did* hate this man. It just wasn't fair.

"Dami-*Ahhhhhhhhhh!*" My back bowed up off the bed as Damien slammed his size into me and I was transported back to that night, ten years ago. Only this time, I knew what to expect and I wasn't delusional enough to believe that Damien Greystone liked me or had any feelings for me outside of loathing.

Well, loathing and lust, apparently.

I opened my legs wider to accommodate his body between my thighs and to relieve some of the sting. He immediately pulled out and rammed his cock back inside my body again. I grabbed onto his powerful biceps as he began his assault on my very soul.

I kept damning myself to hell every time I moaned and wrapped my legs around his waist tighter. His cock was so thick and hard inside me that it felt like it was battering against every nerve ending in my cervix. The pressure and sting felt glorious, but I knew come morning my body would be used up and sore.

My eyes never left Damien's. I wasn't going to let him off that easily. I might have given him permission to use me however he sees fit, but he was going to have to look me in the eyes as he did it. Only it wasn't shame I saw lurking in those green pools. If I believed in miracles, I'd say I saw adoration in them.

Suddenly, I couldn't control all the pleasure, pain, guilt, and heartache that was coursing through my body. I let out a quiet sob and a single tear escaped down the right side of my face.

The only sign of Damien noticing my meltdown was the increased force of his thrusts into my core. He started slamming into me with so much power that I thought the headboard of the bed would splinter. He pushed his arm between my back and the mattress until his hand came up from behind and wrapped around my shoulder, preventing me from scooting up.

Damien held me in place as he pounded into me with impossible might. It was almost as if he couldn't get deep enough inside me to satisfy his craving. There was no way he wasn't going to have bruises on his pelvis. You couldn't batter ram yourself against someone as hard as he was and not walk away unscathed.

"Jesus, baby, your pussy feels like a vise around my cock," he grunted. "I'm going to empty my dick inside you all night until I have nothing left to give you, Halloween."

"Damien, please…" I would deal with the shame later. Right now, I just wanted more of whatever drug he was giving me. I'd never felt so full and so *desired* as I did right now with him slamming into me. He was trying to turn everything I knew about him into a lie, and if I let him, then the shit he did to me as we were children would be nothing compared to the devastation that he could cause me now.

"Please what, baby?" He labored over me and I could see the cords in his muscle straining with his efforts. "You need to cum?"

"Yes…"

"Beg me, Halloween. Beg me to make you cum. Tell me it's *my* cock you want fucking this tight, hot cunt. Tell me and make me believe it, baby."

"Damien, please…." My body was on the edge of another explosion and just needed that final push.

"I said make me fucking believe it," he grunted.

"Damien, just you…only you. Just…please…it's *always been you."* And that was the truth. He made sure to spend our childhoods embedding himself into my every emotion that I'd never get him out.

And I believed that after this, I wouldn't.

He buried his face in my neck and his next words pushed me over the edge. "And it's always going to be me, Fiona."

I came with so much force that white spots danced behind my eyes and my entire body locked up. It seemed as if my orgasm did nothing but spur him on more because he didn't relent at all and kept viciously fucking me through my spasms.

Now, if every romance book I have ever read was to be believed, this was the part where he was supposed to cum with me, and then we'd lay quietly, basking in the minor traumas our bodies just went through.

Well, the books lied because Damien didn't cum.

He. Just. Kept. Going.

And going, and going, and goddamn *going*.

However, it appeared my body was on the same page as Damien's was because my legs instinctively pulled up higher giving him all the access that he needed to ruin me.

And ruin me he wanted. "That's right, baby, give me one more. Give me just one more, and then I'll let you rest."

I let out a confused whimper because my overwhelmed mind knew I needed a break, but my traitorous body wanted none of it.

I started pushing my body towards him and actively fucking him back. He let out a strangled groan and moved his arms to hook both my legs over the crooks of his elbows. I didn't think my body could open more for him, but I was wrong.

I had no leverage whatsoever to hinder the force of his thrusts. His dick was so big that he kept hitting something inside me. It was uncomfortable and sinful all at the same time.

"Damien, I can't...it…it hurts…" It didn't exactly hurt, but it couldn't be good for my insides to be knocked around, right?

He pulled back from my neck to look at me, not once letting up. "Good. I want you to hurt, Halloween. I want every ache and pain you have to result from my cock in your cunt."

I started to feel that familiar build up at his words. Who knew dirty talk could be such an aphrodisiac?

It wasn't five minutes later when my body exploded with that sensational starburst of pleasure. I could feel my pussy clench mercilessly around his dick, and praise Jesus, it was enough to make him lose control.

"Fuck, Fiona." I looked up at him in time to watch his face contort with his release.

Goddamn, the man was beautiful.

He kept thrusting inside me until we could both feel his erection begin to subside, and then he simply rolled off of me to lie beside me.

That didn't surprise me as much as when he slid his arm under my neck and used his strength to haul me up, so that I now had my head resting in the crook of his shoulder, my cheek on his chest. God, why did this feel so comfortable? How could I feel anything…*positive* with this man?

"What now?" I immediately stiffened as those exact words took me back to the one other time that I had said them to him. I just had the best sexual experience of my life and it was tainted with memories of cruelty and broken emotions.

My body was basking in the glorious aftermath of his touch while my mind was screaming at me that I was weak and stupid. My pride joined in, telling me that being broken and homeless was better than betraying my soul and letting this man use me.

Damien stretched his other arm across his stomach to grab the back of my thigh and haul it across his body. He was truly cradling me now, and it scared the fuck out of me.

"You give me five minutes, so that my dick can recover. After that, we'll take a shower."

"A shower?"

"Yeah. It'll be easier to clean you up in the shower after I paint your face and tits in my cum."

CHAPTER 10

Obsession doesn't even begin to cover it now.

Damien ~

It was Saturday morning, and I had my laptop cracked open working in the suite's sitting area. I couldn't sleep and I didn't want to be tossing and turning in the bed, possibly waking Fiona. Still, like the certified creeper I was, I made sure I was facing the bed, so I could glance up every now and again and make sure she was still there, proving that last night had been real.

I fucked her all night until my dick had nothing left to spit out on or inside her, and even then, I would have gladly eaten her pussy and finger fucked her the rest of the night if I had thought her body could take it. However, I had to wake her up the last two final rounds to even get her to participate because her spent body had kept passing out on me.

I kind of felt sorry for her. If I was obsessed with her before, that was nothing compared to the deranged possessiveness I felt now. The high I felt at having my hands on her body, my lips on her skin, and my cock in her sweet mouth and hot, tight cunt was a feeling I would kill to keep experiencing forever.

The site of her in the shower on her knees with her lips wrapped around my dick was seared into my brain. Still, I could admit that I'd been a little half-ass shocked that she hadn't bitten my dick off as soon as I stuck it in her mouth. Lord knows no one would blame her after all the shit I've put her through, but she hadn't.

Fiona had swallowed as much of my dick as she could and-this could be just wishful thinking-she had come off like she was in love with being on her knees before me. She had handled my cock like she'd been sucking me off for years. The finish had been a tossup between looking down at her in the shower with my seed covering her face and dripping all over her big ass tits and later on the bed when she had swallowed every last drop that I had forced her to take. Luckily, I could alternate the endings for the next six months, or hopefully the rest of my life if everything worked out as planned.

It was another hour before I heard the sheets rustling on the bed. I looked up to see the blankets moving about in waves. The next thing I saw was a very confused but stunning face underneath a mess of brunette silk pop up from the bed.

I really had to find a better way to handle everything she made me feel.

I set my laptop aside and strode over to the bed area. "Good morning, baby." I leaned over to kiss her when she planted her hand on my chest and stopped me.

"I've let you do a lot of things to me in our lifetime of knowing each other, but you are out of your goddamn mind if you think I'm going to let you kiss me while I have morning breath." She shook her head to emphasize her point. "Not happening."

I righted myself, but I couldn't contain my chuckle. "I'll grant you a reprieve this time because I know you're still getting used to the idea of…*us*. However, I suggest you learn how to expand your level of comfort around me, because in the future, morning breath, no shower, or even your period is not going to keep me from putting my hands on you, understand?"

She looked so dumbstruck that it actually made me smile. "You…you...you can't…you can't have…" I smiled wider when she lowered her voice to a whisper. "You can't touch me during my *period.*" Her eyes darted around the room like there might be a possibility that someone else may hear her. "It's messy and I'm pretty sure it's unsanitary."

I threw my head back and laughed. It wasn't something I did often, but God love this girl. "Maybe, Halloween. But there's no way I'm going a day without touching you if I don't have to, let alone a week or however long that fucking thing lasts."

She blinked up at me. "You're crazy, you know that?"

"Baby, you have no idea." If she did, she'd run out of here screaming.

She held the sheet closer to her body as if I didn't already know what she was hiding underneath it. "I…uh, I need to go home and-"

I was already shaking my head at her. "I went to the store while you were sleeping. There's a bag in the bathroom that contains everything you need to be *comfortable*. I'll order breakfast from room service while you shower or do whatever it is you think you need to do."

Fiona threw me an evil eye, then wrapping herself up tighter in the bedsheet, she padded her way towards the bathroom…and slammed the door.

I stuck my hands in the pockets of my lounge pants and just stared at the bathroom door. I knew this wasn't going to be easy, and honestly, I didn't deserve for it to be easy. I did a lot of foul shit to her growing up-hell, I was *still* doing foul shit to her. However, if I came clean and told her the absolute truth, she'd have everything she'd need to walk away from me, and I couldn't let that happen.

The absolute truth was that I had been drawn to her when we were five; I had been confused by her when we were ten; I had begun my obsession with her when we were thirteen; I had already been in love with her when we were sixteen; I had already been living just for her when we were eighteen, and now…well, now I'd slit my wrists open and bleed out at her feet if she asked me to. I *loved* this woman like no sane man was capable.

The bathroom door burst open and in her hands was the bag full of evidence that my obsession with her was very *real.* Fiona started grabbing random items out of the bag and pointing them out towards me like it was a show-and-tell. "How did you know to buy all this stuff?"

I just lifted a shoulder at her, not saying anything. She'd just be pissed at the truth.

"Oh, no, buddy," she hissed. "How did you know I use *this* brand of toothpaste, or that this is the *exact* same shampoo and condition I use? You even have the same damn deodorant, Damien."

God, she was magnificent when she found her backbone. "It's not important-"

"Oh, I think it's very important, Damien. So, unless you want me filing a restraining order the second that I leave this room, I suggest you tell me how you know all this shit about me."

Sadly, the truth would do nothing but cement the fact that she *should* get a restraining order. "I broke into your house and wrote down what you use."

The bag dropped out of her hands, and she stood there rooted in shock. Her mouth opened and closed a few times before words finally made it through. *"You broke into my house?"*

"How else was I supposed to find out what you used?"

"How about you wait until I wake up and *ask* me, you lunatic?"

"But then you wouldn't have had all the things you needed when you woke up." Admitting I wanted to take care of her had me feeling stupidly awkward. I was Damien Sebastian Greystone III. I didn't do awkward…unless it came to Fiona Eldstead, apparently.

She dropped her head and tightened the sheet she was still wearing around her body. She mumbled something, but I couldn't quite catch it because she was so far away from me. At least, it felt like she was too far away from me.

I crossed the room, and putting my finger under her chin, lifted her head, so I could look into her sweet face. "What was that, baby?"

"Don't be nice to me," she whispered.

Even though her words were slicing me open, I understood her meaning. She was used to me being cruel to her, and she preferred that treatment because…well, the devil you know and all that. It was when I treated her like she mattered that twisted her up and I wasn't entirely sure how I could fix that.

I cradled her face in my palm and bent to kiss the side of her neck. "You gave yourself to me for six months, Halloween. I can treat you however I want to."

She let out a quiet moan as I continued to kiss my way down her neck, and it was a lost cause after that. I yanked the sheet out of her grip and pulled it down the middle. The move was so unexpected that she didn't have time to secure her hold on it. Fiona was standing gloriously naked in front of me and since I was only wearing the pair of lounge pants, I had them shoved down and her legs wrapped around my waist before I even had her back pressed up against the wall.

I knew she was sore and swollen, but that didn't stop me. Maybe that made me a complete asshole, but I could always justify my actions towards her by reminding myself that she just simply made me crazy.

My cock was so hard that when I went to ram myself inside of her, it forced her to open and take me. "Damien!" Fiona threw her head back, and like a man dying of thirst, I latched onto her exposed neck taking her skin in between my teeth and marking the fuck out of her.

She had random bruises, bite marks, and hickeys all over her body from last night, but I had made an effort to leave her neck untouched because I respected her position as a business owner and example to her employees. Still, the act of Fiona opening her body to me not a minute after she asked me to stop being nice to her had me all fucked up.

She had me all fucked up.

Just her existence has been wreaking havoc on my mental and emotional stability since we were fucking five goddamn years old.

Fiona didn't pull away or ask me to stop marking her, so I sucked on her neck as I pounded my cock into her swollen tightness. I could vaguely hear her body slam repeatedly against the wall every time I pushed into her, but again, she wasn't asking me to stop or protesting about any pain she may be feeling, so I kept attacking her body with mine.

"Damien, don't stop. I'm close. Please, don't stop," she begged me, and the sound of her breathless pleas had me nearing the edge with her. I dreamed of this.

"Take it, baby. Just keep taking my cock." I held off long enough to feel her heat start clenching around me, making me feel like I was man enough for her.

I wasn't ashamed to admit that when we were naked, my masculinity was directly tied to whether or not Fiona climaxed. My obsession demanded that she be so sexually satisfied that it would never occur to her that another man could give her something I couldn't. I had no problem with her telling anyone that would listen that I was a cold, heartless bastard of a dick. But there was no way she'd be able to say I didn't satisfy her in bed and not be lying.

"Oh, God, I'm cumming…" she screeched, and I followed immediately after.

We stayed as we were for a few seconds as we both came down off our highs. I reluctantly pulled out of her and placed her on her feet. I didn't miss the wince on her face as I did.

I pulled up my pants, and then I picked up the offending bag that had fallen at her feet. Grabbing her hand, I walked into the bathroom, and after placing the bag on the counter, I pulled out the bottle of bubble bath I had bought her. I made my way over to the oversized tub and ran the water as hot as I thought would be bearable, and then poured some of the bubble bath in.

When I turned around to place the bottle on the counter, I noticed Fiona looking at me with that constant stunned expression on her face. "What's the matter, Halloween?"

She shook her head. "Nothing," came her low whisper. I ran my eyes over her body, and I counted it as a small victory that she was comfortable enough to stand before me completely naked.

God, I loved her body. She was everything I wanted my woman to be. She was soft with tits I could get lost in for days. Her stomach wasn't six-abs flat, but it was flat enough that I could watch her tits bounce as I ate her pussy. She had wide hips that could take a pounding, and thick thighs that held on tight when she wrapped them around me. Fuck, I've been craving this body of hers since we were thirteen, and now that I had it, I would do everything in my power to keep it.

I grabbed her by her hand again and walked her over to the tub. I removed my pants and got in first. I stared up at her until she got the message.

She dipped her foot in first and immediately pulled it back out. "Holy shit, Damien, the water's hot as hell."

I smirked at her. "No, it's not. Quit being a wimp and get in."

Her eyes narrowed at me calling her a wimp. She dipped her foot in again, and this time she hissed as she slowly sank down in front of me. I secretly wanted to shout out an exclamation in victory when she leaned her back up against my chest and settled in.

I wrapped both my arms around her just underneath her tits and held her body to mine and just laid my head back on the end of the tub and savored this moment.

"I can't believe you're not burning up."

"The water needs to be hot, Fiona, so it can ease some of your soreness," I explained. Even though I wouldn't fault her, I didn't want her thinking the hot water was another way for me to torture her.

She let out a quiet, "Oh."

We sat like that silently for a while before she spoke. "You know, none of the nice things you're doing for me will change that fact that I hate you, right?"

I wish I could say I knew she didn't mean what she was saying, but I couldn't. I had no doubt she meant every word she just said to me. "I know."

"So, then, why do it? I mean, why be nice to me? We both know I'll do whatever I have to in order to keep you from sending my parents to prison, so why bother with the niceties?"

I tried not to wince at the mention of sending her parents to prison. I hated that she really believed I'd do that to her, even though I would. But I couldn't win her without extortion, so she had to keep believing it until she started feeling something for me other than hate.

"You're confusing me being nice to you with me doing what needs to be done in order for you and your body to be at my disposal, Halloween. That bag on the counter is just a bunch of practical shit I knew you were going to need. I have you for only a few more hours before I have to go back to San Francisco, so I'm not going to waste them with you going home to shower."

She got really quiet for a second, but then asked, "And the bubble bath?"

"Like I said, I only have a few more hours with you today and I plan on spending them inside your cunt. I need your body available for my cock, so if I have to pour a goddamn bubble bath for it to be able to accommodate me, then so be it."

God, I was such a fucking bastard.

CHAPTER 11

There aren't enough meds in this asylum.

Fiona ~

It wasn't often that Vicky was rendered speechless, but her shock was very real. I quickly wondered if I was going to have to throw a glass of water in her face to shake her out of her stupor.

"Sweet Baby Jesus, Fee. Are you for real?"

I signaled the bartender for another round. "Yep. I couldn't make this shit up if I tried, Vee. I don't have that good an imagination."

"Okay, first I call bullshit on the imagination. I've seen your drawings and paintings. You have a wonderful and beautiful imagination."

I snorted. "Maybe when it comes to landscapes and portraits, but not when it comes to a childhood tormentor moving away to become a multi-millionaire, only to come back for the sole purpose of extortion and blackmail over the fat girl's body in order to keep her parents out of prison." I took a good, long gulp out of my fresh beer before continuing. "Do you think my mind's creative enough to come up with that Twilight Zone shit? Because it's not, Vee. It's really not."

She grimaced. "For the millionth time, you are not fat, Fee. You're voluptuous and hot as hell. If I swung that way, I'd totally be wining and dining you to get into your panties." The weirdo winked at me.

"Thanks, Vee. That means a lot to me." I leaned over and kissed her cheek.

"So, you really called Jason and told him you couldn't see him anymore?"

"Yes, and the phone call had been horribly uncomfortable."

"I bet. Talk about where are the psych meds when you need them."

After Damien and I had gotten out of the tub, he had carried me and sat me on the bed. He then walked over to my purse and had pulled out my phone. I still remember vividly the sinking feeling in the pit of my stomach when he had handed me the phone.

Damien had stood over me in all his naked glory as I had explained to

Jason how I thought it was best that we stopped seeing each other. Naturally, he had asked for a reason since we had been getting along so well with our casual relationship. However, I hadn't had an answer, except for the truth, and I sure in the hell wasn't going to tell him that. In the end, Damien had saved-or damned me-when he had plucked the phone out of my hands and had told Jason that I couldn't see him anymore because I was now fucking him. If Jason had anything to say about it, I wouldn't know because Damien had instantly hung up on him after that.

Then had turned off my phone.

I waved after the bartender again. "Hector, can we get a couple of shots, please? Our usual." He nodded his acknowledgment and went to pouring.

Vicky was still trying to get a handle on the clusterfuck I just dumped in her lap. "So, then all you have to do is sleep with him for the next six months and your parents are off the hook, then he goes back to San Francisco and you go on living your life like before? Without Jason, of course."

"Yep."

"Here you go, ladies." Hector placed the shots in front of us along with a bucket of beer. Hector was a great bartender. As soon as I had ordered the shots, the man knew Vee and I were making a night of it.

"Have you heard from him since he drove back to San Fran?"

"Nope." I hadn't heard from him since he'd driven back Sunday night and here it was, already Wednesday. "I think it's all part of his twisted game. He always did enjoy making me a nervous wreck."

"So, the plan is to get shitfaced and then…?"

Luckily for me, Vicky had chosen a career in creative web design. She worked for a company based out of San Francisco, but she worked mostly from home, thus making her the perfect friend to have in a crisis. She could get drunk with me on demand.

"I don't know yet. I offered Debbie a thousand dollars to cover for me tomorrow, but being the sweet girl that she is, she agreed to do it for her regular overtime rate. However, if I need to get drunk again tomorrow night, she's taking the thousand dollars."

Vicky held up her shot glass towards me. "To fucking hot multi-millionaires."

"Seriously, Vee? I was thinking more of along the lines of to buying new identities and moving to Istanbul."

"Okay, this first shot will be to Istanbul, but the next one is definitely going to be to fucking hot multi-millionaires."

I was too caught up in my pity party to argue, and so we both threw back the shots of tequila. God, the burn felt stupendously like the beginning of a night of bad choices.

We set our empty shot glasses down on the bar and went back to our beers. "Promise you won't hate me if I ask you something?"

I side-eyed her. "If I was ever going to hate you, it would have been when you set me up with on that blind date with Todd Morgan."

"Good point." Vicky mashed her lips together clearly remembering the disaster of a date that she set me on. "Okay, so you've told me everything about this wrist-slitting play, except for one thing. You haven't mentioned if Damien's good in bed or not, Fee."

I could feel the heat creep up my neck. Some people might think her question was invasive, but to me it wasn't. Vicky has been with me since we were five and has stood by me through every humiliation I have ever endured at the hands of Damien or whoever else had chosen to be cruel to me during my years of living. I never felt shame or embarrassment with her.

"As long as you don't hate me for answering honestly," I countered.

Her eyes rounded and her brows arched high. "Like I could ever."

I closed my eyes and confessed my greatest sin. "God, Vee…there are no words. *None.*"

She squealed and her smile took over her entire face. "Oh, my God, oh, my God…I *knew* it."

Now that she's gotten it out of me, I couldn't stop sharing. "He's built like a goddamn Greek god, and he has this tattoo that's…well, I don't know what it is because he didn't let up on me long enough to study it, but it covers his right shoulder and fades down his bicep and right pec. It's soooo sexy. He's strong and fit all over. He's fucking stunning, Vee."

"Yeah, yeah, yeah…his package, Fee. What's the size of his man package?"

I laughed. "His man package? Really, Vee?"

"Fine, what's the size of his dick?"

I instantly scanned the bar and area around us. "Will you keep it down?" I hissed.

"I bet that's not the first time since Damien's been back that you've uttered those words," she smirked.

"I hate you. I mean, this time, I mean it. Not like all those other times." I deadpanned.

"Answer the question, Fiona, before I really make you hate me."

And of course, I answered because Vicky wasn't one to make empty promises. "As wide as my wrist and as long as a cucumber," I divulged.

"Like a full-grown cucumber or one of those ridiculous baby cucumbers?"

"Full-grown. Like, collecting social security grown."

We sat silently drinking our beers as Vicky digested that tidbit. The only reason I wasn't walking around with a limp today was because I had taken a hot, hot bath every night since Sunday. The ache was barely beginning to fade.

Women who claim they want a man who can fuck them all night long have clearly never had a man who *has* fucked them all night long. It wasn't a matter of desire so much as a matter of biology. Unless you were a porn star and have conditioned your body to have sex for hours on end, your body will shut down from exhaustion and overuse.

The final round before he had left Sunday night had been more pain than pleasure. I had been so swollen that he'd had to force himself inside me. I wasn't talking about alpha male aggression force, either. I was talking about my body closing off to his invasion. Damien had to finally go down on me and make me cum twice before he could slide inside, which reminded me that I should probably buy some lube.

"It's so unfair," Vicky finally spoke. "Why do all the assholes get to have big dicks and fuck like gods? I mean, it's just not fair."

I could only nod in agreement because it really wasn't fair. "I'm in so much trouble, Vee. Everything that jerk did to me felt like I'd let him touch me forever." I dropped my head on the bar. "What is *wrong* with me, Vee? How can I enjoy his touch after everything he's done to me? Hell, after everything he's *doing* to me? I'm fucking him to keep my parents out of prison and all I can think about is how he makes my body feel. I must be sick in the head."

Vicky's face softened. "Awe, Fee, I wish I had a genuine helpful answer for you, but I don't. There's a reason the phrase 'I'm going to fuck you like I hate you' exists. Sex isn't always tied to love. Hell, it's not even tied to hate sometimes. People have sex for all kinds of reasons, most of which don't include a loving relationship. You think because your body craves his touch that you're betraying your parents or maybe even betraying yourself. He doesn't deserve your pleasure or your forgiveness, but…"

She trailed off, and I knew it was because I wasn't going to like where she's going with this. "But what?"

"I love you, Fiona, so what I'm about to say next is not a dig at you in any way, okay?" I nodded for her to continue. "I know Damien made your life hell growing up. I know it better than anyone as your best friend all these years with court side seats to the shit he did to you, but you never told on him. You never asked your parents to switch schools or go on independent study. You never made one effort to put a stop to it. Have you ever asked yourself why?"

"Because I was a pussy?"

"But you weren't. It was only Damien you never stood up to and I think it's because, deep down, you were afraid that your parents or our teachers would make him actually leave you alone and you secretly didn't want that." She lifted a shoulder and drank from her beer. "I think that as twisted as your relationship with Damien was, it was still a relationship to you. I mean, why else would you give up your virginity to him so easily? I think it's because, in your mind, you guys had been dating since you were five-years-old, that's why. Why do you think you gave in so easily, even now?"

I brought my head back up off the bar at that question. "What do you mean? He threatened to send my parents to prison, Vicky."

"Yeah, and instead of responding like the grown, mature business owner that you are, you gave into him without a fight just like on graduation night.

Fiona, you could have threatened to call the cops and charge him with extortion, but you didn't. I think you need to really evaluate how you feel about Damien Greystone. Forget that you're supposed to hate him, and then tell me what you feel when you're with him."

"Oh, and how exactly do I do that when he makes me feel *everything?*" I turned to Hector. "Hey Hector, can we please get another round of shots?" If I thought I needed tequila before, this conversation was definitely making me need it now.

"My honest opinion-"

I snorted. "Does anyone get any other kind of opinion from you? Ever?"

Vee side-eyed me. "Shut it, woman. My honest opinion is that I think you should use this…thing, this arrangement to exorcise your Damien demons. Let yourself feel whatever it is you feel around him and maybe when the six months are up, you'll finally be able to really move on. You'll finally be open to a real relationship with a guy because you'll no longer have residual feelings over a boy from your childhood."

"So, Ann Landers, what happens if I end up falling in love with him and he walks away at the end of six months anyway?" Hector placed our shots in front of us and I wasted no time downing mine.

"Then you will have loved him, and he will have broken your heart, but you get to *move on*, Fiona. You nurse your heartache like all the millions before you who have had their hearts broken. Fee, you have six months to find out why he treated you the way he did. You can finally get some real answers. You need this." She polished off her shot following her advice.

I was so goddamned confused. "You think?"

"I think, Fee. And if nothing else, you walk away from this having the best sex of your life. I say you use his cucumber until it rots."

I wrinkled my nose. "That's not a very flattering image, Vee."

"What do you want from me? I'm not the one with a creative mind, you are."

I could only stare at her. "Vicky, you work as a creative web designer, hence the word '*creative*'."

She waved away my logic. "Potato, pahtahto."

"That makes no sense. *You* make no sense." I opened another beer fully prepared to take responsibility for the hangover that would kick my ass tomorrow.

"Look, I can't remember the last time I got laid, so if you have to spread your legs for the both of us, then that's what you're going to do." She yelled for Hector. "Hector! We need more shots, please."

"Are we getting you laid, then? Is that what this shot is heading towards?" I needed to know the game plan. I was a great wing-woman like that.

We gave Hector our undivided attention when he delivered our shots. "Are you ladies going to be okay? It's not even eight…" He raised his brows in silent reprimand.

Vicky pointed at him. "You're a bartender, Hector. You're not supposed to judge. However, because you are, I'll have you know I haven't gotten laid in over three months. Count them, Hector…*three.* So, if we want to get drunk and pick up random dick, you should be supporting us in this, not being all judgey."

Before Hector could respond, a voice came from behind us that almost instantly killed the buzz I had worked so hard for. "As long as you're the only one picking up random dick, Vicky, then you have my full support. However, Fiona's in possession of all the dick she's going to be getting for the next six months."

Just my luck.

Damien fucking Greystone.

CHAPTER 12

If she could only see inside my mind…or maybe not.

Damien ~

The drive back to Fiona's was tense.

Probably because I was pissed as fuck.

When Andrews had texted me and told me Fiona and Vicky were at Mercury's getting drunk, I saw red. I cancelled the rest of my afternoon meetings and had driven the hour drive in forty minutes.

Even though I had commented to Vicky that I was in support of her treasure hunt for random dick, I hadn't been. After lecturing her on the idiocy of her night's plans, I'd gone on to inform her that she must have been extremely stupefied by drink if she thought for one second that I was going to leave her drunk in a bar to be picked up by some random guy. I had given her two choices, either get into my car quietly and allow me to drop her off at home, or I could carry her out of the bar and child lock her in my car.

She knew better than most that I didn't make idle threats, and so she had chosen the former option.

Fiona didn't say anything as we got out of my Mercedes. She didn't say anything as I stood behind her while she unlocked her front door. She didn't say anything as I walked into her kitchen and poured her a glass of water.

Her house was a small cottage-style home. It boasted of a living room that blended into the kitchen. It had two bedrooms that were separated by a single bathroom. It was modest, but it was cozy and roomy. I actually liked that none of the furniture matched. Fiona had a home, not a house.

She hadn't moved from the living room and just eyed me as I handed her the water. "Here, drink."

She took the glass, drank the water, then finally spoke. "How did you know I was at Mercury's?"

I decided to tell her the truth. "I've had a private investigator reporting to me on everything you do since the night I crawled out of your bedroom window."

If my phone were out, I'd take a picture of her face. "Wh…what? You're lying. What? *Why?*"

I shrugged a shoulder. "When I got home that night and had to wash your blood off me, I realized we hadn't used a condom. I needed to know if you had become pregnant or not."

"You're lying," she accused, again. "Even if that is true, why would he still be following me *ten years* later? And don't for one second think that I believe that you gave a shit if I became pregnant or not."

Her words had me seething. I was aware that I'd been a giant prick to her for all those years, but to accuse me of being so low that her getting pregnant wouldn't have fazed me…well, that was bullshit. I stepped closer to her. "You really believe that I wouldn't have cared if you had gotten pregnant with *my* child?"

She put her hands on those fuckable hips of her. "Oh, I'm sure you would have cared. It probably would have upset you to have to take money out of your clothing allowance for the abortion, no doubt."

I grabbed her by her arm none too gently because I just couldn't help it and shook her to make my point understood. "Make no mistake, Fiona, had you ended up pregnant as a result of that night, you'd still be married to me now with at least three additional Greystones following in the wake of the first."

She never struck me as the violent type, but here she was, pummeling my chest with her all-mighty fists. "Don't lie to me! Quit lying to me, Damien! You're such a fucking asshole!"

Even though she wasn't doing any damage, I grabbed her wrists and held her still. "Stop it! I realize you're drunk and probably feeling braver than you normally would, but I'm telling you now, I won't tolerate your nonsense for much longer!"

She yanked herself out of my hold so hard that I was surprised she didn't fall back onto the floor. I stood there as she righted herself up. The look she shot me was lethal. "Why?"

I stuck my hands in my pockets to keep myself from reaching for her. "Why, *what?*"

With her anger spent, there was only one other emotion left in her drunken stupor and it almost brought me to my knees. She wasn't sobbing hysterically, and honestly, I wish she had been. Hysterical crying, I could chalk up to drunk girl emotions. However, this calmness as tear after tear just poured from her eyes had me wanting to slit my own throat.

Fiona looked like her heart was actively breaking with every second she stood there. "Why do you hate me so much, Damien? What could I have possibly done to you at five-years-old to make you hate me so much? Just...ple…please, help me understand why…wh…what I did?"

I stood there silently staring at her, wanting to kick myself in my own nuts. I wanted to lay my soul bare, but she's been drinking, and this wasn't a conversation I wanted to have while she was drunk. This conversation deserved a fair chance, and it wouldn't get one while tempers and emotions were high and under the influence of alcohol.

She grabbed the empty glass of water off the table and threw it at me. *"Answer me!"*

I didn't move because, let's face it, I deserved her wrath. Still, her aim was shit, so the glass sailed past my head and met its demised, shattering in the kitchen somewhere.

"We're not going to have this conversation while you're drunk, Fiona, so-" I stopped when I saw her frantically looking around for something else to throw at me. I stepped to her and grabbed her by her shoulders. "Stop it and calm down, Fi-"

Her eyes rounded, then she covered her mouth with her hand. I knew that look, and I knew that gesture. Anyone who's ever been drunk knew it well. I jumped back out of her way and watched as she flew past me towards the bathroom.

I was on her heels and found her lifting the toilet lid just in time to empty her tequila shots. I went up behind her and pulled her hair back with one hand while I rubbed her back with my other. I cringed every time I felt her muscle contract. Vomiting sucked, no matter what the reason.

"Shh, baby, you'll be okay."

She hugged the porcelain for ten minutes before it became clear that she was finally done. I let go of her hair and went back into the kitchen to get her another glass of water. I found her exactly how I left her when I made my way back to the bathroom.

I handed her the glass. "Here's some water, baby."

She took the glass and used the water to rinse and swish her mouth out before spitting back in the toilet. She silently handed me back the glass, and I placed it on the counter. Then I lifted her onto her feet and helped her to the counter. Without speaking, I handed her the toothpaste and her toothbrush. She took them both and began brushing her teeth.

I turned on the shower and adjusted the water to her liking. She watched me through the mirror, but still didn't say anything.

I stepped up behind her and bent to remove her sandals. Once those were off, I reached around and unbuttoned her jeans and slid them, along with her panties, down her legs and off her feet. She worked with me in removing her blouse as she was still scrubbing her teeth and tongue. I didn't blame her for brushing her teeth until her gums bled. Did I mention before that throwing up sucked?

She unhooked and took off her bra herself and finally she was standing before me naked. God, this woman made me crazy. I wanted to take that perfectly trimmed triangle she had above her pussy and barber my goddamn name in it. I wanted to tattoo my fucking name across her tits. I wanted her wedding ring to spell out Greystone in diamonds and keep her pregnant every year with fifty kids.

Fuck. The more she let me in, the crazier I was becoming.

I started ripping off my clothes, nearly strangling myself with trying to remove my tie. Her eyes got huge in the mirror. "At ur u oing?"

I lifted a brow. "What does it look like I'm doing?" I didn't stop undressing.

She turned around and gawked at me. "Yo an seousy be urn n rit now!"

I just smirked at her. "I'm always turned on around you, baby."

She turned back around, dropped her toothbrush back in the toothbrush holder, then spat out the rest of the toothpaste and rinsed her mouth out. The second she was done, she whirled back again to face me. "How can you possibly be-" She waved her hand towards the vicinity of my crotch. "-turned on after just watching me throw up tequila shots?"

I stepped towards her completely naked, lifted her by her hips, sitting her on the edge of the counter. "I've already told you…morning breath, not showering, your period, or you throwing up a bar full of alcohol will never keep me from wanting to stick my dick inside your luscious pussy lips, baby."

She looked a hot mess. Her hair was matted, her makeup was a ruined mess down her face, her eyes were puffy, and I could see her gums still bleeding a little bit, but God, she made my heart hurt.

I grabbed her by her hips and scooted her ass to the edge of the counter. I had to bend my knees a bit to make my cock align with her cunt, but I didn't mind. As long as I was inside her I didn't mind whatever I had to do to get there.

"Damie-*oh, God…*"

I stopped whatever she was about to say by slamming my cock into her hot heat. She braced her hands on the counter on either side of her and threw her head back so hard that I was surprised the mirror hadn't shattered behind her. I wanted it to shatter. I wanted her home destroyed in the evidence of my possession of her body. I wanted her house to look like a tornado had come through it.

The more that image ran through my mind, the harder I fucked her. I placed my hands on the inside of her thighs and pushed them back, so she was spread impossibly wide open for me. My gaze left her face, and I looked down at my cock splitting her pussy open over, and over, and over with each thrust.

I reached one hand behind her neck and forced her towards me, so I could plunder her mouth with my tongue. She opened her mouth despite her reservations a few minutes ago and I drank from her.

Christ, I never wanted to stop kissing this woman.

Ever.

I felt her hands grab a hold of my shoulders, her fingers digging into my skin. I could feel the steam from the shower beginning to envelop us as I drove faster and deeper inside her. I grabbed a chunk of her hair and pulled her head back to open her neck to me. I began kissing her jaw, working my way down. "I will always want you, Fiona. There isn't anything you can do that will put an end to my craving for you. Your pussy was made for my cock, baby."

She let out a defenseless whimper as I bit down on her skin. I stopped trying to respect her position as a business owner after the first hickey I had bitten into her neck. I'll just buy her a closet full of scarves. Problem solved.

"We're not getting in that shower until you cum on my cock, Halloween. So, if you still want there to be some hot water left, I suggest you hurry this along."

"Oh, God..."

I made my way up to her ear and whispered, "Play with your pussy, Halloween. Dance those delicate little fingers over that hard, hot clit of yours, baby." I picked up the pace because the image I was painting was sending tingles down my spine.

She jerked back and looked up at me. Her chest was heaving, her body was sweating, and her eyes were clouded with everything she wanted to do but was too embarrassed to do.

I slammed into her hard and deep and kept myself still inside her. "Fiona, baby, before these six months are done, there isn't anything that I wouldn't have done to you or with you. I plan on doing every dirty, filthy, unholy thing I have ever fantasized about doing to you. So, believe me when I say, you playing with your pussy is going to be the least of our offenses."

I leaned in and kissed her soft, perfect lips and started pumping my steel back into her softness. "I'm going to make you love every deliciously depraved thing I do to you because I'm going to make you love *me.*"

Fiona threw her had back again and came so hard around my cock that I thought the tight grip of her pussy was going to snap my dick off. *"Fuuuck…"*

"Damien…" I watched in pride and self-male gratification as Fiona's body twitched and thrashed about on the counter. The vision brought out the insane idea that I could sell my shares of G&C to Will and do nothing but live off the interest of my millions while I spent every waking minute I had inside this fucking woman.

I would never misjudge an addict again for the rest of my life.

I fucked her through her orgasm, not letting up one bit. If I couldn't get her to love me, I would do my best to make her addicted to me.

I picked her up and held her limp body to mine as I finally made our way to the shower. I pushed her back up against the tile wall and continued my assault on her pussy. She wrapped her arms around my neck and did her best to wrap me in her thighs, but I knew she was weak from her climax.

I pinned her to the wall with my chest and held those thick sexy as fuck thighs in my hands. I rammed into her over, and over, and over again until I felt that familiar sensation gathering at the pit of my balls.

I picked up the pace. "I'm going to cum, baby. Your pussy's strangling my cock so hard that it's going to make me pump you full of my seed."

"Yes...oh, God, yes...Damien, cum inside me..." she begged.

Three pumps later, I was emptying everything I had inside her hot, perfect center. *"Fiona."*

She tightened her arms, thighs, and pussy all around me and held on as my cock seemed to twitch endlessly.

After a while, I set her on her feet and kissed her with all the passion that I felt for her. When I pulled away, she was crying. She touched her fingers to her lips. "Damien..." she whispered.

I brushed wet strands of hair from her face. "What, baby?" I whispered back.

"Wh...what was that?"

I wanted to confess everything. I wanted to beg forgiveness for all my previous sins and come clean about what was really going on with her parents, but I couldn't risk her walking away. I needed to cement her to me before telling her the full truth, so I did what I've always done when it came to her and how I felt about her. "That was fucking, Halloween. Had Jason known how to really fuck, you'd know that."

CHAPTER 13

I'm so not cut out for this gig.

Fiona~

Vicky and I sat quietly side-by-side in our massage chairs as our assigned spa and massage associates work on our pedicures. It was Saturday afternoon and our entire day had been spent being pampered, plucked, polished, dyed, waxed, and any other number of tortures you could think of that made up a spa day.

Before Damien had left me pissed, and, oh, so very sated Wednesday night, he had informed me that G&C was having a business meet-and-greet sort of gala Saturday night, and I was expected to attend. I had wanted to decline because rich and powerful was just not my scene, but he had coldly reminded me of my 'girlfriend' obligations when it had come to the agreement to keep my parents out of prison.

I had considered it a small victory when I had insisted Vicky attend with us and he had agreed. I wouldn't know anyone there, and I was not going to be that stupid, unsure, uninterested wallflower while Damien mingled and shook hands on multi-million-dollar deals.

Damien had set Vicky up at The Four Seasons and his executive assistant, Rachel, had set both of us with this over-the-top spa day.

I wasn't going to lie, the pampering had started out luxurious, but once we'd gotten to the plucking and waxing and scrubbing...well, then, not so much.

"Why aren't you removing your birth control and trapping that man into marriage, Fee? These spa treatments alone are worth going to confession every Saturday for the rest of your life." She let out a satisfied moan as her masseuse performed more of her magic on Vicky's feet.

"As Housewives of Beverly Hills as that sounds, I think I'll pass. I was kind of hoping that the father of my children would love their mother, ya know."

I had my eyes closed, so I could only imagine the roll of Vicky's eyes when she responded, "Pfft, puhleeeease, Fee. No man, who looks like that and has money like he does, blackmails a woman unless he loves her."

"That makes no sense at all. Like, none at all, Vee."

"All I'm saying is to not be so quick to dismiss the possibility that he has feelings for you. He doesn't need to resort to extortion or driving an hour back and forth from anywhere to get balls-deep in some pussy. He's extorting *you* and he was driving an hour back and forth for *your* pussy, even before he knew the sex was going to be red-hot."

"The people around us didn't all of a sudden lose their hearing, you know?"

She snorted. "The people around us have heard worse, I'm sure."

Not sure which one since my eyes were closed, but one of the spa employees piped up with a, "We have."

"It's only been a week, Vicky. Can we hold off trapping him into marriage until maybe month three?" I suggested.

"Ugh, fine. But I want to go on the record that I think you're wasting valuable time with that plan. You could be knocking out beautiful little Greystones with black hair and green eyes already."

I couldn't hold in my laugh. This woman was so good for me.

I was still feeling sort of hurt when Damien had dismissed that kiss in the shower as being a part of random fucking. It had really cut me when that he could mention another man to me as his cum was still running down my thighs.

He was playing games with me, confusing me. One minute he would treat me like I was special, saying things like he was going to make me love him, and then the next, he was being cruel and reminding me that I was just an unpaid whore who didn't need reasons or explanations.

And I was too stupid and broken to guard myself against his whiplashing.

Anger was my only shield, but when he touched me, anger wasn't what I felt. Damien was using his command of my body to keep me off balance, and even though I knew that's what he was doing, I couldn't help but give into him. I had spent so many years letting him make me feel bad that I craved how he made me feel good now.

"Well, be that as it may, three months really won't make a huge difference in the scheme of things. Besides, why can't our babies have brown hair and brown eyes?"

Vicky tsk'ed like I was a moron. "Because the world needs more hot, black-haired, green-eyed gods. Quit being stingy, Fee."

She had a point.

We made it back to the hotel around six. Damien had agreed to let me get ready at the hotel with Vicky as long as it was understood that I'd be going home with him at the end of the night. I hadn't mentioned to him that I had never been confused about where I was sleeping-or not sleeping-tonight.

The spa had sent over stylists to fix our hair and makeup, so all we really had left to do was put on our dresses. Vicky had chosen a black baby-doll strapless dress that showed off her toned legs to perfection. She wore a silver raindrop pendant with matching earrings and her jewelry complimented her silver-strapped heels. Her red tresses were pinned up high on top of her head with a cascade of random curls falling around her face. She looked stunning. Redheads weren't a dime a dozen like brunettes and blondes, so she was sure to stand out, no matter where she went. However, dressed as she was, she was going to leave the faint of heart in her wake as she made the rounds tonight.

I had chosen-at the request of a certain overbearing male-a jade green dress that hugged my body as it flowed down to the tips of my pedicured green toes. Damien had requested I wear a dress that matched what he was wearing, but I had wanted to match him, not his clothes, so I had chosen green for his eyes.

The dress was held up by two poor excuses for straps and plunged low enough to show the public what I was working with. It tapered in at my waist, flared out at my hips, and then loosely fell the rest of my length. It was stunning, classy, and expensive.

It was everything I was not. I didn't even have enough sense to bring some jewelry.

"Christ on a pogo-stick, Fiona. You are going to become a YouTube viral sensation tonight when Damien can't take it anymore and finally mounts you at this party in front of God and everyone."

I raised my brows at her. "I doubt it. Everyone will be too busy looking at you in that dress to even notice what Damien's doing to me."

"Ahhh, so you admit there's a chance of said mounting happening, huh?"

I laughed. "Will you be serious for once?"

She shook her head. "Never."

She came to stand next to me in front of the mirror that adorned the vanity room. She looked at me through the mirror. "Fuck that, Fee. We *both* look gorgeous." I smiled at my friend. She truly was the best, and she knew me well. "Fuck those uptight, gold-digging, rich bitches. We're going to walk in there proud of who we are, and ghetto or not, I will throat punch a bitch with a quickness if any of them come at us sideways."

"YouTube here we come."

The knock on the door announced it was time. I needed to stow away whatever anxiety I was feeling because it was showtime.

Vicky followed me and stood behind me as I answer the door to a very stunning and breathtaking Damien Greystone. He was dressed in a customary tux, but it looked like sin and danger on his body. I stepped back as he walked past me glancing quickly at Vicky. I was about to shut the door when a very grownup and hot as hell blonde-haired, brown-eyed William Creston followed in behind Damien. I had been so caught up in Damien's beauty that I hadn't even noticed Will.

Will smiled down at me, and grabbing me by the shoulders, leaned in to kiss me on the cheek like we were long-lost friends or something. "Fiona, it's such a pleasure to see you again." He gave me a friendly once over before returning his gaze to mine. "You look absolutely stunning."

I took an involuntary step back and I knew my face must have looked dazed and confused. Shock made me honest. "Well, I wish I could say the same about you. I mean, while you do look handsome in your tux, it's not all that much of a pleasure to see you again, Will."

He had the grace to flush, and I saw him dart a quick look at Damien before facing me again, but before he could respond to my blunt honestly, Damien snapped, "That's enough, Fiona."

"No, Dame…she's right. Walking in here after all these years and greeting her as if I never had anything to apologize for was an asshole thing to do." He kept his eyes on me as he addressed Damien and his whiskey-colored gaze didn't waver as he continued. "I'm sorry, Fiona. I'm sorry for a lot of things, but right now I'm mostly sorry for treating you as if you're still the weak girl we treated you as in school."

The room was silent at his apology, and I realized that no matter the man he was now, as children, he had been just as caught up as I had been in the hurricane that was Damien Sebastian Greystone. We were all followers back then. Well, except for Vicky. "I accept your apology, William."

His smile was sincere and beautiful. "Thank you, Fiona. And it's Will."

Damien shattered the moment with his abruptness. "You ladies ready?"

"Yeah, we just have to get our bags and shawls. But-"

Vicky finally spoke up. "Wait a second, what's he doing here?" She pointed to Will.

The smile Will gave her fluttered my ovaries. "I'm your date, Vic."

"My date? What the hell do you mean *'my date'?"*

"When Dame told me that you were attending with Fiona, I told him you could be my plus-one."

The look she gave him would have leveled a lesser man. "Oh, did you, now? And the both of you thought this would be a fine idea without running it by anyone first? The 'anyone' being me."

Will snorted at her little women's lib speech. "Asking you would imply that you had a choice, Stems, and you don't. You are my date for this evening, and if you act nice, I may even kiss you at the end of the night."

Damien already had his arms around Vicky's waist, holding her back. "I'll show you what you can kiss, you pompous jerk!"

It took no effort on Damien's part to hold Vicky still. The man was strong and immovable. "Calm the fuck down, Vicky. It's simple; either you attend with Will or you don't attend at all."

"Dame-"

He shot me a look that had no problem shutting me up. "What's it going to be, Halloween?"

Vicky was spitting mad and spoke before I could. "Fine," she spat. "No need to threaten Fiona, Damien."

Only Will seemed to be pleased about all the surrounding chaos. "Great. Can we get going before our guests start to wonder where the G and C of G&C are?"

Vicky mean-mugged him as if he'd just kicked her cat and stomped over to the couch to grab her silver purse and shawl. Will held out his arm, and she wrapped her arm around his so hard that he started laughing at her rebellion. I had been joking about YouTube earlier, but now...hmm.

Damien stood next to me, and we both watched silently as Will and Vicky headed for the suite door. I could hear him let out a deep breath as he reached for my shawl and wrapped it around my shoulders. I went to get my purse when I felt his hands on my shoulders hold me still. He leaned down and kissed my neck just below my ear. "You look so breathtaking that if we didn't have to go to this fucking party, I'd take you home and fuck your pussy over, and over again with you covered in my cum, Fiona. I would rub it into your skin, so you smell like me, even after you shower."

I jerked, swung around, and looked up at him to see if he was serious. The look on his face and the fire in his eyes told me that he was very serious. It made my skin heat and my blood simmer. "You've already emptied yourself on and inside my body. You've left me with bruises and bite marks. You've branded me with hickeys and dug your nails into my skin. I think you've claimed my body enough, don't you think?"

Damien bent himself at the knees, so he was face-to-face with me. He took my face into his hands and speared me with this green stare, making sure he had my undivided attention. "Not even close," he hissed. "I'm nowhere near staking my claim on you, Halloween. If you're not careful, you'll find yourself strapped down to a table, rendered helpless, as I tattoo my fucking name on the inside of your thighs. One will be branded with Damien while the other one will be branded with Greystone."

I gasped at his ridiculous threat. It was a caveman riddled statement, and I knew he couldn't mean it, but it was hot as fuck, nonetheless. And, again, I was questioning everything I thought I knew about his man. Or maybe it was because I didn't know anything about this man. I just knew the boy he used to be.

He stood to his full height. "Let's go. Will and Vicky are waiting on us."

We left the room, and after a very sexually charged elevator ride down, we found Will and Vicky waiting in the lobby for us. Will with a sexy smug decorating his face and Vicky scowling but still holding onto his arm.

Any progress was still progress.

The men escorted us into the limo and discussed business and the guest list of the party. Vicky looked out the window and took in the night lights while I did my best not to succumb to an out-and-out panic attack.

I knew it sounded ridiculous, considering all the man sitting next to me has done, but I didn't want to embarrass him. This was an important party, and it was going to be attended by the most important people of the West Coast and some from the East, and Damien was going to show up with me on his arm.

I felt him reach over and cover my hand with his. I looked over at him and he wasn't even looking at me. He was still conversing with Will about what to expect tonight. I glanced over at Vicky and the hand holding hadn't gone unnoticed by her. She met my stare and gave me one of her heartwarming smiles as she mouthed 'I love you'. I smiled back feeling much, much better.

With my friend by my side, I could get through anything.

CHAPTER 14

She still doesn't get it…all I see is her!

Damien ~

I could tell she was nervous. She had a death grip on my hand the second we walked into the building. The party was being held on the third floor which held our auditorium. The first floor was obviously the lobby. The second floor comprised of two large conference rooms surrounded by eight smaller ones. The third was our auditorium and the rest of the building was made up of floors full of offices with mine making up the entire top floor.

As soon as Will and I walked into the party, whispers started floating in the air and heads started turning. I have spent all my life around the rich and influential and most of them all had one thing in common; they were vain, vapid vultures.

I knew it was going to be a long night, but it had been made longer the second I saw Fiona in the hotel. I didn't know how I was going to get through the night without sticking either my tongue, fingers, or dick inside her pussy.

Will was the first to speak. "Alright, let's do this," he chuckled.

"I have a question," Vicky announced. "Where's the bar?"

Fiona looked at Vicky. "Ooohhh, good question."

Vicky shrugged a bare, smooth shoulder. "I thought so."

Will laughed. "There'll be cocktail waitresses floating about with-"

"Tequila?" Vicky asked. "Because if they're not floating around here with tequila, then I need to know where the bar is, Will."

I could tell Fiona was surprised when Will wrapped his arm around Vicky's waist and hauled her body to his. "Tonight's going to be great." He looked back at us. "See you guys around and about."

I just smirked at Vicky's expression as Will carried her off to mingle and whatnot. "So much for her keeping me company," I heard Fiona mutter.

I kissed her on the top of her head. "You don't need her for company. I'm not leaving your side, Halloween."

I spent the next hour shaking hands, making pleasantries, and wishing the clock would move faster, so I could get Fiona home and out of that goddamn dress.

Fiona had been nothing but perfect since we arrived. She hadn't even batted an eyelash when I had first introduced her as my girlfriend. I had just finished promising Myron Stanley a meeting when I saw Will and Vicky making their way towards us.

I could tell something was up because Will never did dramatic. "Hey, Dame." He spared Fiona a quick glance. "I just ran into Bernard Willis. He's hoping to congratulate you on our West Coast success."

Bernard Willis has been a long-time client of ours and I respected him professionally. Respecting him personally was a different matter. His personal proclivities were questionable at best, and if he was a vulture, his daughter was a buzzard. And if Will was warning me about his approach, it could only mean he brought his buzzard with him.

"I have to go to the restroom and I'm taking Fiona with me," Vicky announced.

Before I could protest, Vicky had already grabbed Fiona's hand and was dragging her away. Vicky was lucky she was Fiona's best friend, or I might have had to kill her.

"How many millions would I have to give you, so that you would let me leave you here to host the rest of the party alone?"

Will tossed his head back. "You don't have that many millions. Besides, Dame, I'm not letting you do anything that's going to keep me from getting inside Vicky tonight. Holy shit, dude. She had always been a pretty girl, but fuck me running, that is one hot redhead."

I didn't blame him. Vicky had grown up to become a beautiful woman. "Fine," I conceded.

I was getting antsy waiting on Fiona when I heard my name being called from behind me. "Greystone!"

I turned around and found myself face-to-face with Bernard and his daughter. "Bernard," I shook his hand, "it's good to see you on the West Coast." I nodded my head at his daughter, Crystal. "Crystal, you're looking lovely this evening."

She smiled her predatory smile, and I wanted to close my eyes and teleport myself to the women's restroom. "Damien, you're looking as handsome as ever." She placed her hand on my arm and I wanted to scrub her touch off of me with a scouring pad.

I did my best to pull my arm back from her without seeming too rude. Normally, I wouldn't give a shit about stuff like that, but I made it a point to never forget that what I did and how I behaved business-wise affected Will as well.

What the fuck was taking the girls so long?

Bernard turned to talk to Will about whatever the fuck, leaving me stuck to entertain the blonde-headed viper standing with us.

Crystal inched closer towards me than I was comfortable with. "You know, Damien, it really is a shame that we didn't get to spend more time together before you came out here permanently."

Where. The. Fuck. Was. Fiona?

"Your father is a very valued client. As much as we try to treat each client as if they're the only one, there are just not enough hours in the day." I stepped back as stealthily as I could.

She pouted and coyly looked up at me through her ridiculously fake lashes. "I wasn't talking business, Damien."

Thankfully, Bernard unknowingly threw me a lifeline. "Enough business for tonight." He elbowed Will in a good, ole boy manner. "Where's that hot redhead I saw you with earlier, Will?" The douchebag winked. "You surely have your hands full with that one. Is she your…uh, girlfriend?"

Before Will could answer, Crystal spoke up in what I imagined she thought was a flirty manner, "Oh, Daddy, men like Will and Damien don't have time for girlfriends. They're too busy ruling the world." She giggled, and I wanted to slam myself headfirst into the nearest wall.

Will held up a finger at her. "Actually, Crystal, that's not entirely true." He winked back at Bernard. "She's not my girlfriend *yet,* but I'm working on it." He shot me a quick look. "She's actually with *Damien's girlfriend,* freshening up. We're just the sad saps waiting out here for them."

Bernard laughed good-naturedly and surprisingly handed out a genuine tidbit despite his slimy ways. "Never forget, my boy, if you're not willing to wait on the woman you love, there's always someone else that's willing to."

Will nodded in agreement. "That's why we're standing here, Bernard."

"Well, we'll let you guys get on with it. See you gentlemen later." He stepped away, but Crystal lingered behind.

The next thing I knew, she was pressing her body up against mine whispering in my ear, "The next time you find yourself on the East Coast, give me a call. Your West Coast girlfriend never needs to know about it." I saw her eyes dart behind me and the smile that stretched across her plastic face told me everything I needed to know about where Fiona was.

She patted my chest. "See you around, handsome," she cooed, and I watched as she walked away from us.

Fuck.

I turned around to see a very pissed off Vicky and a...calm?...Fiona walking towards us.

Vicky wasted no time, only she directed her bullshit towards Will which threw me off a little. She nodded her head in the same direction as Crystal. "If you hurry, you can still get at that, Will. My tits are natural and normal-sized, so I can't, *nor would I,* compete with that."

Will grabbed her by her arm with enough force to surprise the shit out of me. "Don't get it twisted, Stems, if I wanted that, I'd have that. She's not all that difficult to get. I'm here with *you* and I haven't said or done anything to give you the impression that I want to be here with anyone else, so knock your shit off *now.*"

I lifted both brows at him. Their interaction seems a little extreme for a first blind date. Vicky yanked her arm out of his grasp and stood looking livid and beautiful. Will's going to have issues letting her get away, no doubt.

I decided to stop being a coward and looked down at Fiona. She was watching their interaction with the same surprised look that I had. She must have sensed me looking down at her because she turned her attention towards me and...*smiled?*

Crystal was all over me and not Will, but here we were, with Vicky getting in his ass about it and Fiona seemingly unaffected by it all.

"I need a drink and not a classy glass of sophistication you got these servers offering. I'm going to the bar and I going to get a real drink." Vicky looked over at Fiona. "You coming, Fee?"

Fiona laughed. "Of course." She looked back at me. "I'm just going to make sure she doesn't do anything stupid. You guys go mingle and make your millions." She walked over to Vicky. "We'll be fine." Fiona looked at Will. "I promise I won't let her embarrass you amongst your friends and business associates, Will."

Will looked like he was going to say something, but the girls strolled off before he could speak.

I let Fiona go out of wariness more than anything else. She didn't react at all to seeing another woman damn near wrapped around me and that bothered me.

It bothered me a lot.

"What the fuck was that all about?" Will threw his hands up in confusion.

"Does it matter? You're getting on a plane tomorrow morning and going back to New York, so she won't be an issue after tonight." I shrugged a shoulder baiting him. "And if it's about getting laid tonight, well, we both know you don't need her for that."

The look he shot me had the corner of my mouth lifting in a rare smile. "Fuck you, dude."

This time, I let out a full-blown laugh. "Good luck with that, man. You're going to need it."

Will shook his head, flipped me his middle finger, then went off to network.

Everything in me wanted to go after Fiona, but I didn't want to add any more fuel to Vicky's fire. So, I did what I always did when I needed to drown thoughts of Fiona out of my head, I threw myself into my work.

I spent the next hour pretty much the same way I had spent the first hour here, only this time, Fiona wasn't by my side and I felt the difference instantly. I had made an effort to pass the bar area occasionally just to check if they were still there and I wasn't the only one. I noticed Will passing it just as pathetically as I had.

Christ, this shit was fucked-up.

It wasn't until my umpteenth time circling the bar area that I almost lost my shit.

Vicky and Fiona were still sitting in their same spots, but this time, there were two guys chatting it up with them. The group looked happy, fun, and single.

Fuck that shit.

I stormed over to the bar like the unhinged man that I was. I saw Vicky give Fiona a slight head nod, alerting her to the fact that I was baring down on her. She turned back towards me just as I came in behind her, forcing the asshole who was favoring her to move over a bit.

"Having a good time, ladies?" There was enough edge to my voice that I noticed the men suddenly tense up.

Vicky looked me dead in my eye as she responded, "Absolutely, Mr. Greystone." She gestured towards the two men and smiled at me. "We've even managed to make some new friends."

I had every intention of behaving like the rational businessman I faked for the public at large, but when I looked down and saw the bored expression on Fiona's face, I actually felt the stitches that held my sanity together begin to unravel.

I turned to both men and stuck out my hand. "Damien Greystone. And who might you two gentlemen be?"

They each shook my hand as they shared a nervous look. "Mr. Greystone, I'm-"

I waved away whatever Guy #1 was about to say. "Actually, I really don't give a fuck *who* you are-" I stepped up to stand in front of Fiona and making each man have to take a step back. "-so much as I give a fuck about *what* you're doing."

"Dami-"

I ignored Fiona and went full-blown 8th grade locker room on them both. "Innocent or not, stay away from my girlfriend, fellas. Trust me when I tell you that you'll be healthier for it."

One guy threw his hands up in surrender while the other murmured, "Sure thing."

I stood there like a fire-breathing dragon defending its castle as they walked away without saying anything further.

"You had no-"

I shot Vicky a withering look. "Vicky, I am not the one and now is not the time." She looked over at Fiona and that was the final straw. Vicky had every right to hate me, but just like when we were in school, I wasn't going to let her stand between me and Fiona.

After telling the bartender to charge their tabs to the company's expenses, I marched both girls over in search of Will. I quickly explained to Will what happened, and he didn't argue when I told him Fiona and I were leaving. He knew me well enough to know that I wasn't fucking around and seeing Fiona all chummed up with another guy had me holding on to my inner psycho by a thread.

The wait for the limo was quiet and filled with enough tension the valet was acting nervous. The ride back to my penthouse was just as uncomfortable, but luckily for the chauffeur, he had the partition up, so he didn't have to suffer the tension like the poor valet had. However, the private elevator ride was really, really bad.

It wasn't until we passed the entry way and found ourselves in my living room that the silence was finally broken. "What the fuck, Fiona?"

CHAPTER 15

Is there a 'Being in Love with A Psychopath for Dummies'?

Fiona ~

Damien had nerve. I mean, he always had a hell of a lot of nerve, but acting the way he had in the bar, after he just had some blonde tramp wrapped around him, was even beyond what I thought he was capable of.

I dropped my shawl and purse on his couch, then turning to face him, crossed my arms over my chest. "Excuse me?"

He had stripped off his jacket and was working on his tie as he answered. "Don't fucking play with me!" he roared. "What the fuck did you think you were about drinking and flirting with other guys after I just spent the night introducing you as my *goddamn girlfriend?!*"

I couldn't describe what I was feeling. When I had walked out of the restroom and had seen that blonde draped over him, it had felt like my heart had been literally breaking into pieces inside my body. I had wanted to cry because it had felt as if I had just caught my boyfriend cheating on me. It had felt like him walking into Ben Lester's graduation party with Heather on his arm all over again.

But Damien hadn't been my boyfriend then, just like he wasn't my boyfriend now.

We had an arrangement where I fucked him on command to keep my parents out of trouble.

I didn't have the right to be upset, and so I had put on a brave face and had acted as if everything was fine. It had taken a lot of convincing on my part to make Vicky play along with my charade. In the end, I had to remind her of how many times I've been humiliated at the hands of this man. I wasn't going to let him do it again tonight in front of California's elite. So, we had sat at the bar and had pretended like we were at Mercury's without a care in the world. It was going fine until Damien showed up.

"We were just talking and having a few drinks." I raised a brow. "It's not like I had my arms around either one of them whispering in their ear."

He stood there with his hands in his pockets saying nothing and the silence made my insides crawl. He wasn't going to explain what he was doing with her, and he wasn't going to apologize for it.

And I was done being a fool.

My childhood-self was done with wanting her childhood nemesis to like her. My grownup-self was done with wanting to matter to this man after all these years.

I was just done.

I gave a curious glance around his penthouse. "So, where do you want me?"

The look on his face had my heart ready to beat out of my chest. "What do you mean, where do I want you?"

I uncrossed my arms and gestured outwardly around. "Where do you want to fuck me? The couch? Kitchen? Shower?" As I was looking around, I noticed his living room led out onto a balcony. "How about the balcony?" I suggested. "We can give your neighbors a show."

He was in front of me, snatching my arm up, before I could finish with my suggestions. The tick in his jaw was so prominent that I wouldn't be surprised if he cracked a molar. "Did those guys get you so turned on that you're willing to let me fuck you out on the balcony in front of the entire goddamn city?"

I tried to master the art of being cold. I wanted to be disconnected and hard. However, the illusion was shattered as the tears pushed their way out of my eyes and down my face. I wasn't going to back down though, despite the tears. "Of course, not," I snapped. "I'm willing to let you fuck me anywhere there's a surface because that's how a whore is supposed to cater to whoever's paying her, right? And, Damien, I'm no longer confused in the least about me being your whore. Only the payment is my parents' freedom instead of cold, hard cash."

Damien let go of my arm and stepped back from me as if he had been burned. His chest was heaving and the look on his face was pure fury. It was beautiful and frightening.

He was beautiful and frightening.

He regarded me for a few minutes before he spoke, his voice was low and lethal. "Is that how my touch makes you feel? When I'm buried balls-deep inside you, is that what you're thinking? Do you feel like a whore when I'm making you cum over and over again?"

No! I wanted to confess that I felt desired when he was inside me. I felt wanted and needed and sometimes, maybe, loved. But he's gotten enough laughs at my expense over the years. I wasn't about to tell him how I really felt whenever he touched me.

"I understand that it was better for business to introduce me as your date or girlfriend rather than your whore." I shrugged a shoulder as if the realization made me feel nothing. "But either I'm just a whore and available to those guys at the bar, or I'm your girlfriend making you unavailable to the blonde."

"Goddamn it, Fion-"

I held my hand out to stop him. "I get confused in my role when you try to have it both ways, Damien. I can handle the whore part of this deal, but I'm done with the somewhat girlfriend part of it. You can fuck me in private until the six months are up, but you'll have to pick someone else to be your girlfriend in public. I won't do it any longer."

Each word out of my mouth felt like a razor blade across my skin. Vicky had been right all along. I had always felt something for Damien, and it hadn't always been hatred. He had singled me out, and I had convinced myself that it must have meant something. *I* must have meant something to him. However, this arrangement wasn't anything other than a bored millionaire stumbling across an embezzler and deciding to use the connection to me for entertainment purposes.

I had never felt so low and like such a fool as I had when I had walked out of that restroom tonight.

"And if I don't agree to that amendment?"

As hard as I tried, I couldn't keep my voice from cracking. "Then I'll sell Fiona's and my house and hire an attorney if the value doesn't equal enough to pay off the debt."

I could see his entire body lock up at my ultimatum. "She's the daughter of a client whose done business with us almost from the start," he explained, going back to my questions about the blonde.

I told myself I didn't care.

"She's exactly what she appears to be…a gold-digging socialite." He came back to stand in front of me. "I have *never* wanted to, *nor will I ever,* want to sleep with her. That little display was because she took offense to Will mentioning that his date was in the restroom with *my girlfriend.*"

"It doesn't matter, Damien," I whispered. I was emotionally in tatters because of this man. I would be beyond stupid to let his words affect me now.

His next words confused the hell out of me. "Don't do this, Fiona."

I glared up at him, tears still streaming down my face. "Don't do *what,* Damien?"

And then he did his worst. "Fine," he hissed. "If the sale of your parents' assets, your home, and your business equal the amount that your father stole from me, then I won't prosecute on the criminal charges. But if the total is short so much as a *dime*, then your parents are fucked, Halloween."

I stood there and watched him storm out of his own penthouse and I briefly wondered why he was leaving instead of kicking me out. It wasn't until I heard the doors of his private elevator swoosh that I finally broke down in sobs. I curled up on the couch and cried until I had nothing left to give.

After about an hour, I realized I couldn't stay here any longer. I grabbed my purse and checked to make sure I had some cash for a cab, and then made my way to the elevator. My stomach was tied in knots the entire ride down. I was losing everything I worked so hard for and I couldn't even blame Damien for it. Sure, he was the one pushing all this, but there'd be nothing for him to push if my father hadn't stolen from him to support his gambling addiction.

It was almost midnight as I rushed my way through the lobby of the building. I could only hope it wouldn't take too long to flag down a cab. I didn't want to call Vicky because I was pretty sure she was onboard with whatever Will had planned for her tonight and I didn't want to ruin that for her.

I was standing in front of the building, looking up and down the street, when I realized Damien could come back at any moment. I mean, this was his home after all. I took off down the sidewalk looking for a café or all-night diner or something where I could safely sit as I called a cab company or call for an Uber driver.

I found myself about three blocks away when I stumbled upon a cab idling on the street. I approached the side door and knocked on the window. The window rolled down. "I'm sorry to disturb you, but are you available?"

The cab driver looked me up and down before his brows drew down in concern. "Are you okay, ma'am?"

I smiled at him. "I am. I just need to find a hotel for the night, preferably one that won't cost me a payment of my future children." After all, this was San Francisco.

He chuckled a bit. "Sure, honey. Get in."

I got in, and he suggested a mid-star hotel a couple of blocks further down. I started crying when I went to pay but he refused to take my money. "Just get some rest. I promise things will be better in the morning when you've rested and can think more clearly." I thanked him for his kindness and went inside to book my room.

I made my way to my room, which wasn't bad at all, then fell right into the bed, dress and all. The cab driver was right, all I needed was a good night's sleep, and I'd feel better in the morning.

It wasn't moments later that I let the exhaustion take me under.

Suddenly, the unexpected ringing of my phone jerked me out of my sleep. I reached over, and through my sleep haze, I saw Vicky's name flashing brightly at me. "Hello," I croaked.

"Jesus fucking Christ, Fiona! Where in the hell are you?!"

"Uh-"

"Damien has lost his fucking mind, Fiona. He's tearing the city apart looking for you."

I sat up. "I'm fine, Vee. I found a hotel and-"

"What's going on? Why didn't you call me?"

I let out a sigh. "I didn't want to ruin your night with Will and-"

"Fuck that, Fee. I'd much rather be there for you than shacked up with some random dick that I can get anywhere."

I heard a faint 'what the fuck' in the background which I presumed was Will. "Vicky, I'm fine, honestly. I was actually in a very deep and comfortable sleep when you called."

"Oh," she whispered. "Well, text me where you're at before you fall back to sleep, and Fiona?"

"Yeah?"

"I meant what I said about Damien. He thought I knew where you were, and I seriously thought he was going to kill me for not telling him. He really is ripping this town apart looking for you."

"It'll be fine, Vicky. I'll call you in the morning. The *real* morning," I chuckled.

As I hung up, I saw that it was almost two in the morning. "Fuck," I muttered. I fell back onto the bed and prayed I'd be able to fall back asleep. I was just closing my eyes when the pounding at the door shattered all my illusions of a good night's sleep.

It didn't take a rocket scientist to figure out who was on the other side of the door. My suspicions were confirmed seconds later. "Open this fucking door, Fiona, before I break it the fuck down!"

I really didn't want to deal with the police at two in the morning after already having a shitty night, so I threw the covers back to go open the door. I mentally slapped my subconscious when she accused me of wanting to open the door because we were secretly glad Damien came looking for us and not because we didn't want to deal with the police.

The backstabbing, unsupportive whore.

I turned the lock and barely moved out of the way in time before Damien came storming into the room looking like a vengeful god. He turned to face me, and I'd never seen him look this disheveled. His dark hair looked like he'd been running his hands through it all night and his face was dark and livid.

I closed the door behind me and stood my ground. "How'd you find me?"

He stormed towards me, and grabbing my arm, shook the shit out of me. "I will *always* fucking find you, Fiona. I will always know where you're at, what you're doing, and who the fuck you're with. *Always,"* he seethed.

I tried to yank my arm out from his grasp, even though I knew it was futile. "Let me go, Damien."

He threw his head back in a sinister laugh. "You don't think I've fucking *tried?"*

What's he talking about?

"And, so help me God, Fiona, if you ever take off like this again, I'll-"

I pushed at his chest. This man's audacity knew no bounds. "You'll what, Damien?"

He peered down at me and the look on his face had me believing every word he said. "I will buy out everyone in my building and lock you down in the storage basement and keep you down there until we destroy each other. I swear to God!"

Having spent all my tears earlier, now all I felt was rage at his mixed signals. "Well, seeing as how I'm handing over everything that I own to you, I fail to see where we'll find ourselves in this situation again. You can go to hell, Damien. And once I hand over that check, I never want to see you ever again."

He grabbed hold of my other arm and slammed me up against the wall. "That's not how this is going to go down, Halloween. You're going to see me every day for the rest of your fucking life if I have anything to say about it."

I got back up in his face…well, as much as my five-two could against his six-three. "But you don't have any say about it. I'd rather lose everything I own than be your goddamn toy!"

"You're not my fucking toy!" he roared down at me.

"Then what am I?! Jesus, please, Damien…why are you doing this to me? Why can't you just let me have a peaceful, normal life?" My voice began to betray me, and I hated myself for it.

The bottom of my stomach fell out when he answered. "Because I've been obsessed with you since we were five and I still can't control it twenty-three years later. It's *always* been you."

CHAPTER 16

It's not enough…everything is just not enough.

Damien ~

Fiona stared up in shock at my words and I couldn't blame her.

I couldn't begin to describe the panicked sensation I felt when I had gone home and couldn't find her anywhere. I also knew I was losing it when I had actually threatened Vicky with bodily harm. I was not my father, and I knew I had to put an end to all this when I found myself starting to act like him. It was time for the truth.

Well, some of the truth.

"What are you talking about?" she whispered in disbelief.

I let go of her arms and stepped back from her. *Fuck.* I was so not equipped for this shit. I was used to taking without reservation. I normally never had to explain myself. I shrugged a shoulder. "I'm obsessed with you. I always have been. It's the reason behind everything I've ever done to you."

She shook her head, trying to will my words to be lies. "That's…that's…that can't be."

"Oh, I can assure you it can because it is."

I could see all the fight physically leave her body as she slumped back against the wall. "I don't understand. I-"

"Are you unfamiliar with the definition of the word 'obsessed'?"

She shot me a withering glare. "Quit being an asshole, Damien. Of course, I know what the word means. What I don't understand is what *you* mean by it."

I took another step back and jammed my hands into my pockets, but I held her stare. "You made and make me feel things that no other person on the planet ever has. I'm not going to try to explain the feelings you invoke because I can't. But believe me when I tell you that everything that I have ever done has been because of you or related to you in some way."

"You need to leave." She stepped away from the wall and headed towards the door, presumably to open it and push me on through.

I grabbed her by the shoulders and anchored her back against the wall. "I'm not leaving and I'm not letting you leave me. Well, not until you've heard me out." *Like fuck I was going to let her leave me.*

I could see her wrestling with herself. Her face gave away everything. "Fine, but you better make it quick. It's past two in the freakin' morning."

"Give yourself to me for six months and I'll stop-"

She stomped her foot and if I weren't in the middle of making the deal of my life, I'd laugh. "I already agreed to give you six month-"

"Stop. Let me finish." I gave her a pointed look, and she zipped it. "I want six months of actually dating with you. No past, no parents, no jail time, no extortion, none of it. Be with me for six months like we're a real couple, and if at the end of the six months you still hate me, then I'll let you go." I wouldn't, but she didn't need to know that.

"Why?"

"Because I wasn't lying when I said I was obsessed with you. I need to see what I can be with you without all the hate and games. Maybe if the reality isn't what I've always fantasized, I can finally shake you and move on." I was lying, but I was desperate.

Her face was the most sincere I had ever seen it when she spoke, "You don't deserve the chance to cure yourself of me. Not when I'm so damaged by everything you've done to me."

I could only nod because she was right, but I needed a plan. The first plan of force and extortion had fallen apart, so I needed her onboard with this one because I didn't have a Plan C. "True. That's why I'm *asking* you for the chance instead of threatening to ruin everyone you love for that same chance."

"So, you're essentially asking me to be your girlfriend, like an actual girlfriend where we go to the movies and dinner and crap like that?"

"Pretty much." She didn't answer immediately, and I could feel my body turning cold with the realization that she was mostly going to call my bluff on ruining everyone she loved.

"Okay."

Fiona's acceptance was uttered so softly that I had to ask her to repeat herself. "Can you repeat that? I'm not sure I heard you correctly."

She squared her shoulders like she was going into battle and met me head-on. "I said, okay. I'll be your girlfriend for the next six months and…try to…I'll just try."

I took her face in my hands. "Thank you, Halloween."

"Why do you call me Halloween?"

"That's a story for another time. I need to get you back to my place," I answered. I wanted to get her in my bed as soon as possible, and hopefully the psychopath in me won't tie her to the bedposts. She agreed to give this a chance, and I had to find a way to trust that. And her.

I didn't know why, but she had been sleeping in her dress, and so all she had to do was put on her shoes and grab her purse. Once we got to the lobby, she checked herself out, and I ushered her into my car that was parked in front of the hotel. I was lucky enough not to get any tickets, not that I would have given a fuck. My priority had been to find Fiona, and once I had, a parking space was not going to keep me from getting her.

When we finally made it back to my place, it was just about three in the morning. I was used to working around the clock hours, so being up this late wasn't that big of a deal to me. Still, as soon has Fiona's feet hit the carpet of my bedroom, I could tell she was exhausted.

I wrapped my arms around her. "We'll take a quick shower, and then we'll sleep, okay?"

I felt her nod against my chest, and so I picked her up and walked her into the bathroom. She stood silently next to the shower door as I adjusted the temperature of the water and jets. Fiona was so much shorter than I was that I wanted to make sure none of the jet streams would hit her face.

I placed my hands on her shoulders and turned her around in front of me and fucking *finally* had the pleasure of unzipping her green dress. One of the sexiest visions in the world was watching the back of a woman's dress slowly open and treat you to the sight of the soft, feminine arch of her back. Never underestimate the high that undressing a woman could give you.

Once the zipper was completely down, I gently pushed the straps over her shoulders until the dress fell into a puddle at her feet. I stepped back and took in the sight of Fiona in a pair of white lace panties only. I hooked my fingers on the waist of the white lace and pulled them down off her body. She silently stepped out of them, and after tossing the scrap of fabric aside, I turned her around to face me.

She looked up at me through her lashes and I wanted to drop to my knees and pledge to worship her for the rest of my days. I knew she had body image issues, but if she could see herself through my eyes, she'd walk around naked all day knowing the power she'd wield over my sanity.

God, I loved this woman, and it was moments like these that I wished I could tell her.

I reached for the buttons on my shirt when her delicate little hands reached over and stopped me. "Let me." I dropped my hands and stood there as Fiona undressed me and it was the most erotic moment of my life, except for our graduation night. No matter how sloppy, hurtful, and juvenile that night had been, it will still always be the best night of my life.

By the time she was done, my dick was rock hard. She didn't comment on it as she took my hand and guided me towards the shower. She didn't say anything when I reached for the shampoo and she noticed it was her brand again. Maybe the shock was wearing off now that I had confessed my obsession to her.

I went through the entire process of bathing Fiona, from washing and conditioning her hair to scrubbing the soles of her feet. When I was done, she returned the favor and this small experience we were sharing as an official couple had me reeling. It was like I finally had everything I had ever wanted, but it still wasn't enough. I wanted to consume this woman.

We finished showering, and after drying her each other off with towels, Fiona padded her way back to my bedroom and I silently followed her. Things weren't tense or awkward, more like tired and anxious. I knew where I wanted to go from here. Hell, I'd marry this woman tomorrow if I thought she'd go for it. The hesitation and anxiousness were coming from her. I had no problem giving her time to adjust, though. I've known for twenty-three years that she was it for me, she was still new to all this.

I pulled back the covers on the bed for her and all I could think as I watched her slide into my bed was that she didn't belong anywhere else. I wanted her to feel the same way when I was in her home and in her bed.

I crawled in behind her, and call me a pussy, but spooning with her made me feel as if all was right with the world. I guess I was too wrapped up in the moment because I the next thing I heard was Fiona complaining.

"Umph, Damien…I can't breathe."

I instantly loosened my hold on her. "Sorry," I mumbled.

A few minutes passed in silence and her breathing was so steady that I was certain she had fallen asleep, but she hadn't. "Are you awake," she whispered.

"Hmmmm…no," I whispered back.

She took me by completed surprise when she rolled over, pushed me onto my back, and then straddled her luscious body over mine.

The look on her freshly scrubbed face was one of hope. She looked as if she didn't want to be anywhere else in the world. Or maybe that was just my wishful thinking.

She was propped up on her forearms with her face only inches from mine. I ran my hands up and down the sides of her waist just reveling in the feel of her soft womanly curves up against my hard planes. I leaned up and nipped her lower lip. "Aren't you tired, baby?"

"I am." Her eyes kept roaming my face, looking for what, I didn't know. She started planting soft kissing on my face and neck and I wondered how I survived this long without knowing what it was like to be on the receiving end of Fiona's love and affection.

The thought was instantly clouded with images of her doing this with Jason. The darkness threatened to take me under until I heard her yelp. "Damien."

I uncurled my hands from her waist and started smoothing the ache. "Sorry, Halloween, I just…" I didn't know what I was, but I was fairly certain she was making me lose my mind.

She must have known something was up because when she went back to kissing me, she did it vocally. "I am tired, but I want you more, Damien. God, I want you all the time," she confessed.

I grunted and ran my hands up her back until they were tangled in her hair, pulling her head back, making her neck vulnerable to my need to mark her. "What do you need from me, baby?"

She moaned as I tightened my grip in her hair. "Hmm…just you. I need to feel whatever you want to do to me. I need to feel what *only you* can do for me" I leaned up and bit into her neck, sucking the fuck out her tender skin. The harder I sucked, the louder her moan became, and then she was rubbing her slit back and forth across my hard dick.

I let go of her neck once I was satisfied that she'd be wearing my teeth marks for days. I maneuvered her head, so that she was looking back down at me. Her eyes were clouded with lust and her face was flushed with the heat of her blood. She looked so damn beautiful that I almost let those three little words escape my mouth, but instead, I brought her lips down to mine and instructed her between kisses. "Ride my cock, baby."

I felt her sensitive, wet pussy lips pressed further over my dick as she slid back and forth with a little more force. "Oh, God, Damien, I love the way you make my body feel."

I knew better than to believe anything anyone said during sex. The words of praise, love and need were usually said in the name of the actual sex act itself and not the person you were with. Still, because Fiona had reduced me into a lovesick puddle of pathetic, I chose to believe everything she was saying was because she wanted me and not just my cock.

I lifted her hips, and because her sweet, addictive cunt was soaking wet and my dick was hard as steel, her body swallowed me up with little resistance. Fiona threw her head back and let out the sexiest sound I have ever heard.

I was expecting her to sit up and enjoy the show of her huge tits bouncing as she rode every last hard inch, but she surprised me when she remained lying flat against me and began moving her hips back and forth slowly, keeping me deep inside her.

This woman's simple existence has tortured me damn near every day of my life, but the torture she was inflicting upon me now was one of the greatest pleasures I have ever felt. Those three little words kept fighting to get out, but I didn't want to ruin the moment. If I told her that I loved her now, she would either freak the fuck out or think I was bullshitting her, and this was too important. This was the first time she's initiated the sex and the first time that she's let me inside her when she wasn't spitting mad at me.

I. Was. Not. Going. To. Ruin. This.

I held onto her and moved with her hips to reach that spot inside her. "That's it, baby, take it however you need it."

Fiona dropped her head on my chest. "Jesus, you feel so good inside me, Damien." She lifted her head and held my gaze as she upped her tempo a bit. "I want to hold on to my grudge and hate you so much but, Christ, you feel so fucking good. *So fucking good.*"

I couldn't help myself. I tightened my hold on her hips and I started thrusting upwards into her. I kept slamming her body down on my cock until she threw her head back and screamed my name. The second her tight, little pussy started convulsing around me I emptied myself inside her.

She slumped down over me, and we stayed like that, with me rubbing my hand up and down her back, until she slid off me and curled herself into my side.

I was never going to let this fucking girl go.

Never.

I'll be dead first.

CHAPTER 17

I don't know whether to be flattered…or scared.

Fiona ~

"So, you guys are dating now?" I peered up at Vicky over my cup of coffee.

I had slept most of Sunday away, not waking up until way past noon. Will had dropped Vicky off, and now we were hanging out at Damien's-where I proceeded to tell her everything-killing time until he took us back to Smithtown. Damian had driven Will to the airport to catch his flight back to New York.

"Yeah, I suppose we are. Tell me the truth, Vee. On a scale of one to ten, how stupid am I?"

"Are you kidding me? He's packing a wrist-thick cucumber that's obsessed with you. Girl, I'm about to call MENSA for your club membership because any woman that can land a man who's hot, rich, and has got a big cock is a fucking genius," she snorted as we laughed.

"Well, speaking of hot cucumbers…how does Mr. Creston measure up in the vegetable aisle?"

She gave me a sly smile. "Let's just say if he were to call me the next time that he's on the West Coast, I'd answer." The satisfied woman winked at me.

"Oh, so you browbeat me into details, but that's all I get from you? You're a horrible best friend, I hope you know."

She leaned across and set her coffee down on the coffee table, then got comfortable on the couch. "Okay. The man has at least eight inches of Holy Mary, Jesus, and Joseph and can fuck like he's been conditioned all his life to deliver female orgasms. Is that detailed enough for you?"

"Wow." I'd say that was super detailed.

She nodded. "I know. And you know me, I'm not easily impressed. However, William Creston can lay it down like nobody's business." She groaned. "Oh, God, and then he's got these tattoos that just…" Vicky shook her head. "I gotta tell you. There is nothing sexier than watching a man undress and seeing tattoos emerge from beneath his ten-thousand-dollar three-piece suit or tuxedo. I was ready to jump him as soon as I saw the little splash of color peek out from his left wrist."

I knew exactly what she meant. "I know. The first time I saw Damien shirtless and saw that he was decorated in ink, it was enough to make me forgive him anything. I can't think of anything hotter than the male body tatted up." I gave a little shiver for effect.

"Okay, cucumbers and tattoos aside, are you really okay with dating your childhood tormentor?"

I put my almost empty coffee cup next to hers. "I'll admit that I may have agreed a little quickly, but I was just so tired of all of it, Vee. Plus, I thought about what you said, about this being my chance to finally get some answers. I don't think I need an apology because, let's face it, no 'I'm sorry' can erase the past and the mark it left on me. Still, maybe if he explains why, I can…I don't know, heal?"

Vicky side-eyed me, reading my face. "What's really bothering you, Fiona?"

I sighed and dropped my head against the backrest of the couch. "Agreeing to give him a chance, after all he's done to me, is making me feel so weak-willed. I know it's not a fair comparison, but I feel like those battered women who keep forgiving their batterers and going back for more." I turned my head towards my best friend. "I feel guilty and ashamed every time I enjoy him, Vee."

She sighed. "You need to ask him why he was so mean to you back then. His answer might help you with those feelings. Besides, Fiona, you're not that poor, insecure girl you were back then, so quit acting like it. This is not high-school-Fiona dating high-school-Damien. You guys are both grown, successful adults and, yeah, you guys have an ugly past, but Fiona-now can handle whatever Damien-now throws at her." She reached over and squeezed my leg. "I know that for a fact, Fee."

I sat up again. "You think?"

"I *know.*" She shrugged a shoulder. "And if he starts acting like an asshole again, cut off his dick and tell him to kiss your ass."

I winced. "You don't think cutting off his dick might be a bit extreme?"

"Hell no. While I may be encouraging you to see this through, I haven't forgotten everything he's ever done to you," she huffed. "If he hurts you again after all these years, then he deserves to get his dick cut off, then have it fed to wild pigs, so there's no hope of reconstruction surgery."

"Jesus, Vee, wild pigs? Do you even know where we could find wild pigs?"

"No, but that's what Google's for."

"Uh…I'm pretty sure feeding severed penises to wild pigs was not part of the idea concept in creating Google."

"Do you know that for sure?" Vicky countered.

"No, Vee. No, I do not." Her logic could still astound me after all these years.

"So, then, you can't say it wasn't." Before I could respond, I heard the swish of elevator doors opening. I twisted my body and tilted my head a bit to see who it was, even though I knew it could only be Damien walking in here.

I wasn't going to lie to myself. Watching him walk into the room all male-masculine-presence-like had my lady bits tingling. I turned back to Vee and hid my smile as her eyes rounded to ridiculous proportions when Damien leaned down and kiss the top of my head on his way to the kitchen.

"Am I interrupting?" he called out.

Vicky turned her upper body to look over at him. "No. We were just comparing yours and Will's dicks to various vegetable products."

I leaned around her just in time to see Damien choke a little on the bottled water he had pulled from the refrigerator. *"Jesus Christ."* He flicked me a quick glance before looking back at Vicky. "There weren't any other topics you guys could have chosen from? No current events or latest fashion styles?"

I couldn't see Vicky's face, but her voice was smooth as liquid steel. "We could have chosen to talk about how much of an asshole you were to Fiona all throughout school, but we chose to talk about your dick instead of how you *were* a dick." She twisted back around to face me. "But we can pick that topic up if you're uncomfortable with the current one."

I tried to stifle my laugh when Damien muttered, "No. No, your current topic is fine."

Vicky just raised a victory brow at me, and I did laugh then.

Damien came and sat on the back of the couch behind me and started rubbing my shoulder with one hand. "What time did you ladies want to head back?"

Vicky answered for the both of us. "Actually, now would be kind of nice. As much as I'd love to hang out in a penthouse all day in my pajama pants, I got shit I need to do."

I looked up at Damien. "Yeah. I need to get to bed early tonight if I'm going to be worth anything tomorrow at work."

I could see by the tick in his jaw that he wasn't happy about taking us back so soon, but he didn't give us a hard time about it. "Okay, no problem. What time do you get up in the morning for work?"

Both of my eyebrows shot upward. "Are you trying to tell me you don't already know the answer to that? Your PI must not be that good after all."

I could hear Vicky snort laugh before Damien got all Damien on me. "Actually, I do already know. I was just trying to be a good, normal boyfriend and avoid pointing out my stalking tendencies."

I rolled my eyes. "This thing between us will never be normal, so moving forward I can take just about anything other than lies. Don't ever lie to me, and we'll be fine."

"Alright, I'm going to gather a few things, and then we can be on our way." I watched after him as he headed towards his bedroom.

As soon as he was out of sight, Vicky leaned in and whisper-yelled, "Fee, something's not right with that one."

I shot her the most incredulous look. *"Ya think?"*

"No, I mean, I'm serious," she insisted. "That man looks at you like he would walk into oncoming traffic if that's what it took to make you happy, Fiona." Calling me Fiona always meant she was serious. "Damien looks at you look he is in *love* with you."

"You're being ridiculous," I whisper-yelled back at her.

She shook her head. "Don't get confused, my friend. The look in that man's eyes is not one of obsession, it's one of *love.* It's almost as if…I don't know. Like, now that he has permission to be your boyfriend, he's letting his guard down. He's finally free to show you his real feelings."

Before I could reject her assumption, Damien returned carrying our travel bags along with another much larger suitcase. "What's that?"

"It's only an hour's drive from Smithtown to the city. Since you get up at five to open the shop at six, I figure that's plenty of time from me to get back here by nine."

"It's only an hour drive if there's no commute traffic, Damien. It'll take you the full three hours to make it back here in the morning. If you don't feel like taking us home, and then driving back, we can rent-"

He put his hand up to stop me. "No. I'm taking you girls back, then spending the rest of the day with you. Being able to slip inside you tonight is more than worth the three-hour drive back in the morning."

I couldn't stop the blush that spread through my body. "Damien…"

"Fuck, that's hot."

I shot Vicky a side-eye.

Her eyes widened all innocent like. "What? It is."

Damien decided to put a stop to the madness. "Okay, that's enough. Let's go, ladies."

We made our way down to his private parking area in the garage below the building, and after climbing in his car, we started our journey home.

The hour drive wasn't bad at all. I had started to wonder how we were going to approach this whole dating thing when he worked the hours he did, and we lived an hour away from each other. And that was without traffic. The morning commutes into the Bay Area was just as bad as living in Los Angeles.

Maybe the distance could be viewed as a good thing. I already felt overwhelmed by our new roles that maybe not seeing him every day might help me keep the balance I needed in my life. I had a feeling that if I let him, Damien would take over my life and I would never be at his mercy like that again.

Ever.

We dropped off Vicky at home and it felt like such a relief as Damien pulled into my driveway. There was nothing like coming home. I waited until Damien opened the car door for me before I got out. I learned quickly that he was a stickler for manners. I would never have guessed it with how he had treated me as children, but the grown man before me made sure he opened my doors, carried my bags, pulled out my chair, and anything else that had died out in the 50s. And if he was just trying to make up for treating me horribly when we were younger, he was doing a great job so far.

He followed me into the house and immediately headed for the bedroom to put away our bags. The comfort he exuded in my home made me both smile and feel uncomfortable. I couldn't shake Vicky's words about Damien being in love with me.

I walked in the bedroom behind him and sat on the bed as I watched him unpack my bag first. "I can do that, you know."

He didn't stop what he was doing as he responded. "I've no doubt you can, but why don't you go take a shower or bath and relax while I take care of all this."

"I've recently discovered that showers and baths are much more relaxing if someone's in there with you to wash your back," I flirted. I mean, I was actually flirting with Damien Greystone. It was just so unreal.

Damien stopped unpacking my bag and came around to stand in front of me. He dropped to his knees in front of me, forcing me to have to spread my legs to accommodate him. He wrapped his arms around my waist, and while I still had to tilt my head a little bit, we were pretty much face-to-face. But the knowledge that this powerful, rich, strong man would be on his knees for me had my female self-esteem riding a high that rivaled heroin use. "You need someone to wash your back for you?"

I wrapped my arms around his neck. "No. I need *you* to wash my back for me."

He lifted the corner of his mouth in a smirk. "Good answer, baby."

My phone started ringing in my purse and the sound of the personalized ringtone made me sigh.

"What's wrong?" he asked as soon as he saw my demeanor change. "Who's calling?"

I gave him a smirk back. "What, you don't already know?"

"Okay, smartass."

I gave him a pointed look. "Seriously, Damien, at some point we're going to have to talk about the PI you claim you have watching me."

He kissed me on my forehead. "I know, Halloween. And we will, but for right now, why don't you tell me who's calling."

I gave him his reprieve. "It's my mom's ringtone."

Damien got up off his knees and sat down on the bed next to me. "What's going on?"

I hung my head as I explained, "I haven't spoken to either my parents in over a week."

I could feel Damien tense up next to me. "Why?"

"When they told me about the…the, uh, money they owed, I told them I wasn't going to help them, and my dad slapped me when I said they were shitty parents for asking me bail them out."

Damien jumped up off the bed and started pacing back and forth. "That sonofabitch *hit* you?"

Shit. "He didn't *hit*, hit me," I clarified. "He slapped me."

Damien stopped in his tracks and the look on his face was pure outrage. "What the fuck is the difference, Fiona?"

"Well, a hit is like when you swing with your fist like in a real fight. A slap, well it's a-"

"It's goddamn abuse, no matter if it's a hit or a slap, Fiona. And I don't give a fuck that he is your father, *no one* touches you. Do you hear me? *No fucking one!*"

"Damien, calm down. I'm fine. You-"

"Sit down, Fiona. I have a story to tell and you're going to fucking listen," he interrupted.

Well, hell.

CHAPTER 18

She still doesn't get it; Part II.

Damien ~

I didn't want to have this conversation, but she deserved to know why I treated her the way I did all those years. This was going to suck, but if anyone deserved to see my skeletons and scrape me raw, it was this woman.

"I know everyone in school thought I had the perfect life. My parents had lots of money, I was a straight-A student, the sports, Yale, and all that, but my life was not perfect, by any means." I looked down at her sitting next to me and I could see I had her complete attention. It was almost as if she'd been waiting all her life to hear my story.

And maybe she had been.

"My father used to beat on my mom. He might still, but I wouldn't know since I haven't spoken to either of them since I ruined my father's empire and never looked back."

She gasped in shock. "Damien, you don't have-"

"Shh, baby, yes, I do." I've treated this woman like dirt, and she was still giving me the best pieces of her all these years later. I sure as fuck did not deserve her, but there was no way in hell I was going to ever let her go. "I wish I could say it was because he was a mean drunk, or he did drugs, or even that he had an uncontrollable temper, but it wasn't. He was ice-cold, and he demanded perfection from his wife and son at all times. Whether it was dinner being late, a speck of dust on the floorboards, a wrinkle in his tie, my mother's fingernail polish chipped…whatever, she would be at the receiving end of whatever was handy." Fiona brought her hand up to her mouth in a silent 'oh', her eyes glistening a little. "It's okay, Halloween, you don't need to cry for me, baby."

"Damien, I just never imagined-"

I shook my head. "No one could or did."

"Did he ever hit you?"

"No, and it wasn't until I got older that I realized it was because I went to school. It was too much of a risk that a teacher or coach would notice bruises on me and start asking questions." God, I didn't realize how hard this was going to be and it wasn't because I was embarrassed. It was because, as I listened to myself speak, I realized my home situation had never been a good enough reason to treat Fiona the way I had. As a child, it seemed legit enough, but now, as an adult, I saw that it really hadn't been.

"Are you okay? You don't have to finish if-"

I grabbed her hand and held it in mine. "No, I'm fine." I gave her hand a quick squeeze. "Anyway, when I was finally old enough, I had stepped in to defend my mother one night and she actually turned on me."

Fiona gasped. "What do you mean, she turned on you?"

"She started yelling at me, telling me to mind my own business. She said her marriage was between her and her husband, and if I didn't want to get shipped off to boarding school, I'll mind my own business from now on." Even now, all these years later, I could still remember the shock I felt at her words. Why would a woman ever *choose* that?

"She said *what?!*" Fiona shrieked and I loved her more for it.

I chuckled at her outrage for the teenage me. "I'm going to tell you something and I don't want you to freak out on me, okay?"

Her beautiful brown eyes rounded, but she just nodded, giving me permission to continue.

"If I had been a better son, a stronger male, or maybe just a more compassionate person I would have tried to save her again, but I didn't." I didn't know how to tell her this next part without her freaking out or calling me a liar, but I went on anyway. "I was eleven-years-old when my father stood there livid as she threatened to send me away for interfering, and uh...by then, I had…uh, shit…" I shook my head at how ridiculous I was back then and how I kind of still was. "By then, I already had you so under my skin that the threat of being sent away and not being able to see you every day worked. I loved my mother, and it did irreparable damage watching my father use her the way he had, but I needed to be around you more than I needed to save my mother."

Fiona's watery eyes rounded at my revelation, but she didn't comment on it the way I thought she would. "Why would your mother put up with the abuse over what's best for her son?" she asked. "I don't understand."

"Money, Halloween. Money, cars, houses, furs, diamonds, you name it, and it was worth the beatings she endured. It was worth whatever damage it was causing her son. That's why I took everything from them when I was in the position to. Revenge is a motherfucker."

And just when I thought she was going to ignore what I said about her, she piped up again, "Why do you call me Halloween, Damien?"

I gave her a small smile before I leaned over and kissed her on her forehead. "Some of my earliest memories are of my father striking my mother, so I already had a lot of dark emotions in me, even at the age of five.

The older I got, the more I realized frustration at the helplessness of my situation was what I felt the most. The first time I laid eyes on you…" I let go of her and ran my hands through my hair. There was no way she could understand what she made me feel, so she was probably going to think what I was about to say was bullshit or crazy. And, yeah, it may very well be crazy, but it definitely wasn't bullshit. "The first time I laid eyes on you, I finally felt something different from the frustration, fear, and sadness. You made me feel…capable."

I stood up and started pacing. I was getting frustrated at trying to explain how she made…*makes* me feel. "It's hard to explain because I was only five and didn't understand the feelings I was experiencing at the time. You made me feel like I was strong. You made me feel like I could be my favorite superhero, but for some reason, instead of a positive superhero like Superman or Batman, you made me feel like a horror movie villain. When I looked at you, you made me want to be a masked Michael Meyers or Jason because I knew enough about their characters to know that *nobody* fucked with them. You made me feel powerful. You made me wish it was always Halloween, so I could dress up and pretend to be so dangerous that no one would dare come after me. You had made me feel like I was strong enough to go home and protect my mother. You had made me want to protect *you."*

I looked over at her and the tears were really flowing now. "Damien," she whispered.

"You made me feel untouchable when I knew it wasn't true. I knew my father could crush me. So, I began to hate the hope you made me feel, and I started to hate you. Only I didn't really hate you. I never hated you. I just didn't know how to exist around you and how you made me feel," I finally confessed to her.

I sat back down next to her. "As we got older, your hold on me tightened and you had no idea what you were doing to me. You'd go about your day without any need for me and it *killed* me. It killed me knowing that you could and probably wanted to live your life without me around, but I would lose my shit if I didn't see you at least once a day." I let out a pathetic laugh. "You should have seen the state I used to fall into whenever you would stay home from school sick or whatever."

"I don't know what to say," she whispered.

"There's nothing to say." I stood up again and looked down at her. "Look, I know all this sounds crazy and paints me as unstable as fuck, but it's the truth. I wanted to keep you behind me and let no one else see, hear, or touch you. If anyone else realized how special you were, they might try to take you from me, and then I'd really lose my mind," I kept confessing.

Fiona blinked away her tears. "I can't believe how clueless I was all those years."

I sat back down and leaning forward, rested my elbows on my knees as I held my head in my hands. "I was so sure I had given myself away the night I went after Dennis Franks. I'd never felt so much rage as I had that night when I saw him with his hands on you."

"The night you kissed me," she confirmed.

I looked over at her and brought my fingertips to her lips. "Yeah, the night I kissed you."

"Do you have any clue how confused you left me that night? One minute you hated me and the next you were kissing me with everything you had. It was overwhelming," she admitted.

I gave her one of my rare smiles. "Baby, if I had kissed you with everything I had, you would have been naked underneath me that same night instead of two years later."

She lowered her eyes, unsure. "All those girls…"

Fuck. "All those girls were Will's crazy idea of helping me control my obsession with you. After that night with Dennis, he finally understood the depths of my issues with you. He thought if he paraded other girls in front of me, it would help. Hell, we were sixteen-year-old hormonal boys, it should have worked, but it hadn't. Nothing ever did."

"Wow. I just...that's a lot to take in," she quietly whispered as she let out a heavy sigh.

In for a penny, in for a pound. "Well, there's more."

She let out a genuine laugh. "Well, by all means, don't stop now."

"Graduation night was a first for me, too," I confessed as well.

She was so shocked that I had to reach out and grab her before she slid off the bed. I planted her firmly back in place and finally let out the laughter bubbling inside me at her expression.

"You, you…you…" She shook herself out of her stupor. "You were a *virgin* that night, too?"

"Yep."

"No way. No fucking way, Damien," she denied. "You were Damien Sebastian Greystone, the most perfectly hot guy in the entire school. There's no way cheerleaders and other girls with pulses weren't throwing themselves at you all day."

"Every girl but the one I wanted," I confirmed.

"You…you were waiting for *me?*"

I let out a sigh because she still wasn't getting it. "It was always going to be you, Fiona. There was no way I wasn't going to experience that with anyone other than you. I don't think you truly get just how fucked-up in the head I was and still am over you."

"The heartbreak I experienced that night was almost unbearable, Damien. It took me *years* to get over it. It's like I was waiting and waiting for you to come back and make it right, but you never did. I finally had to move on and try with someone else," she brokenly whispered.

"I wish I could tell you I'm sorry and mean it, but I can't. Fiona that night with you is the single most important night of my life," I told her, willing her to believe it. "It's the best of all my life's experiences and I will not lie to you and tell you if I could go back that I'd do that night differently because I wouldn't. I'd still manipulate you into giving me your virginity and I'd still slam my cock into you like I did without any fanfare." Her eyes were so full of disbelief. "Did you know I took a condom with me that night?"

She shook her head. "No."

"I did. Even though I knew what I was going to do, I still wanted to protect you and take care of you while doing it, but my need for you that night was so unbalanced that I'd forgotten to put it on. I almost went crazy knowing I was leaving for Yale and that you'd be left behind, so I had finally gotten the bright idea to put a PI on you. I don't think I could have left if I hadn't."

"You know this is all so…unreal, right?"

I nodded. "Yeah, I know. And I also know that none of what I just told you makes up for how I treated you, and the point of telling you wasn't to do that. I told you all this, so that you'll understand why I plan on having a talk with your father."

"Wait, what?"

"Fiona, I wouldn't stand by and let a random stranger hit a woman in front of me, you think I'm going to just let the fact that your father struck you go?" I snorted at her naivety. "You're out of your mind if you think I'd let anyone put their hands on you and not do anything about it. No one hits you. *Ever.* Your father is not excluded from that."

Her strike was deadly, but she was entitled to it. "So, only you're allowed to hurt me?"

I reached for her, and grabbing her by her hips, straddled her over my lap. I wrapped my arms around her back, keeping her anchored upright. She immediately put her arms around my neck and held on. She also never averted her gaze. That was one thing she never faltered at. No matter how mean I was to her, she always looked me in the eye as she took my abuse. Fiona was a lot stronger than she gave herself credit for. "Yes, only me, Halloween," I confirmed, although my plans were to never do anything to ever hurt her again if I could help it.

She didn't say anything at first. She just kept looking at me like she could see inside my soul and couldn't decide if I was worth saving or not. "Why?"

"Because as we move forward, there are going to be times where I'm working late and forget our anniversary." Her face paled at my words, but I kept going. "There are going to be times where I won't notice you cut your hair or miss one of the kids' soccer games. I'm going to hurt your feelings over the years, but you're always going to forgive me when I do."

"I am?"

"Yes, you are, baby. Because when I'm not unintentionally hurting your feelings, I'll be trying my best to make sure you're happy, healthy, and very, very satisfied." I buried my face in her neck and just inhaled her scent. "I'm going to make sure you never go without and I'm going to do everything and anything I can think of to make sure you don't regret being with me ever."

I pulled back and looked into this lovely woman's face. Her eyes were filling with moisture again and I knew there was no way I could hold back any longer. "I love you, Fiona. I have always loved you and I will always love you. I haven't lived a single day since I was five years old not loving you and I don't want to know what it's like to live a day without loving you. *Ever.*"

She dropped her head onto my shoulder, and tightening her arms around my neck, she sobbed and sobbed. I didn't do anything but sit there and hold her as she cried uncontrollably. I didn't expect her to say it back. I was just finally relieved that I could finally say it to her at all.

CHAPTER 19

I never stood a chance.

Fiona ~

I sat in my office being utterly useless. It was Thursday afternoon, and I was still in a daze from everything Damien had confessed on Sunday. I'll admit I could have reacted with a little bit more decorum but hearing him tell me he loved me, and had always loved me, had pushed me over the edge of everything I ever thought was normal. I hadn't known what to feel about his declarations. It had been a lot to take in, and I was still spellbound over it all. To finally have answers to everything that had plagued me for years was uplifting and scary.

When my sobbing had finally subsided, Damien had drawn me a bath, and I had soaked in the tub while he put all our stuff away and had made dinner. I had been so spent from everything that had happened over the weekend that I had crawled into bed around seven that evening. Damien had joined me in bed, and while I would have gladly submitted to him, he hadn't made a move to have sex with me. He simply held me, and we had fallen asleep together. I think it was his way of trying to prove his words of love to me. As much as I would have loved to have been taken by him, deep down, I knew it had been the right decision.

The next morning had been surreal as we both got ready for work like we'd been doing it for years. We had fallen into a comfortable silence and it was actually nice. I hadn't seen him since that Monday morning, and I didn't know if he was really too busy to make the drive or if he was trying to give me space. I suspected it was the former. Damien hadn't become a multi-millionaire by slacking off.

I couldn't complain, though. Damien made sure to call me every night before I went to sleep. No matter what he was doing, he would take the time to make the phone calls happen. We would talk about our days and our plans for the weeks, normal things like that. And without fail, he'd tell me he loved me before hanging up. I've yet to say it back, but I knew what I felt. The fear of the too-good-to-be-true was the only thing holding me back, honestly.

A knock at the door brought me out of my reverie. "Yes?"

The door opened and a very sexy, very delicious looking Damien Greystone walked through. "Hey, baby."

Surprised, I stood up and made my way around the desk. "What are you doing here?"

He let out a small laugh. "Do you think I've stayed in San Francisco every night because I was too tired to make the drive to you?"

I wanted to play coy, but after all the honesty he shared with me on Sunday, I figured he deserved the same. "I just thought you might be really busy with G&C being so new to the West Coast, and then it crossed my mind that you might be giving me space." I lifted a shoulder. "I don't know."

Damien grabbed my hips and sat me on top of my desk, standing in between my legs, smirking. "I've given you *ten years* of space, Halloween. That's the last thing I plan on giving you, baby." He leaned in to give me a kiss. "I've been working long hours this week, so that I could drive down today and work from home tomorrow."

The words 'work from home' filled my stomach with butterflies. However, I was finding that they were the happy kind of butterflies instead of the usual anxious ones. "I don't want to burden Debbie at the last minute, but I can put in a half day tomorrow."

"I didn't do it to disrupt your day, Fiona. I have no problem waiting at home for you. I have no problem waiting for you for anything." He kissed me again. "I came straight here from work. I can go home and unpack while you finish up your day if that's okay with you." It was sweet how he was trying to respect our new relationship by asking me and including me in his decision-making. We both knew he wouldn't have a problem breaking into my house again. And the fact he'd rather spend time with me in my little home rather than that stunning penthouse of his made my heart lurch.

"That'll work. I'll do my best to get out of here as soon as I can."

I expected a quick kiss and an 'okay I'll see you at home', but instead, he walked over to the door and locked it. He stalked his way back towards me and my body was already heating with the blatant lust lurking in his eyes.

Damien made his way back in between my opened thighs. "I just want to give you a little incentive to get home as quickly as possible, Halloween."

I bit my bottom lip. Ever since he told me the meaning behind why he called me Halloween, it gave me a slight thrill every time he called me that now. Knowing I made him feel powerful enough to slaughter anything in his path made my female self-esteem feel just as powerful. Having influence over something-*someone* so powerful was definitely a high I could get addicted to.

Instead of flipping my skirt up and taking me where I sat, he grabbed my ankles and turned me to face the back of my office. He took hold of my hips and dragged me to the edge of my desk as he sat in my chair. *Holy Mary, Mother of God.* He needed the chair because he was going to feast on me.

And I couldn't wait.

He held my brown gaze in his green one as he spread my legs, opening me up to him. "I've been craving the taste of your pussy for three days, baby." I shivered. "I sit in those boring ass meetings all day, dreaming of how many ways I want to lick your cunt and make you scream."

I couldn't sit up any longer. I fell back, bracing myself up on my elbows, while I let my head fall back, offering up my body to him. "Damien..."

"I can't wait to get you like this on *my* desk. Every day I want to start out my morning with memories of you bent over my desk. I want to sit at my desk and relive staring down at you on your knees while you suck my dick clean."

My body was catching fire from the inside. I loved how filthy he could be. Some women didn't like being spoken to like that and I got it. They tend to think it's insulting and degrading. Not me, though. As long as he treated me with affection and respect outside the bedroom, he could slut-talk me all he wanted inside the bedroom. Or shower. Or kitchen. Or where the hell ever.

Because the gods had decided to bless me this morning, I had chosen to wear a skirt, and I was glad as hell that I had. Damien reached up underneath me and pulled my panties down my legs. I lifted my head back up in time to see him stuff them in his pocket.

He flipped my skirt up until it bunched over my waist and my pussy was open for anything he wanted to do to me. "I missed this pussy, baby."

I lifted a brow. "Just my pussy?"

He smirked back. "I missed the woman it's attached to more, but she has to already know that."

Before I could respond, he sat in my chair and dipped his head, running his hot tongue long and slowly through my dripping wet slit. My elbows crumbled under me and I fell back onto the desk. I reached down and tangled my hands in his dark strands when he took my clit between his teeth and nibbled. "Oh, God."

I felt the cool air hit my center as he used his fingers to spread my lips open for his tongue. The alternating sensations from the cool air and the heat from his mouth had me out of my mind with pleasure. I wanted him to live down there with everything he was making me feel. "More, Damien. Please, I need more."

He spoke in between the licks and the bites. "You want to cum, baby?"

"Yes..."

Damien immediately slid two fingers into my desperate heat and worked that magical spot as he continued the assault on my clit. I could hear how wet I was as he slid his fingers in and out of my body. I should feel somewhat embarrassed that my pussy was so soaked for him, but I didn't have room for any emotion, except the pleasure he was gracing me with.

He worked his fingers harder, and I could feel the clenching begin with my impending orgasm. "Cum for me, baby. Cum in my mouth, so the taste of your pussy can keep me company until you come home."

Oh, God. "Damien…yes…"

He upped the tempo on my clit, and soon, I was cumming with white spots dancing behind my eyelids. He didn't let up, though. He finger fucked me through my convulsions as he swiped his tongue all around my entrance, lapping up as much cream as he could.

I looked up to find Damien with the biggest smile on his shiny face. I watched as he took my panties out of his pocket and wipe his mouth with them. Fuck, everything this man did was hot as hell.

He reached his hand out, and taking my hands in his, pulled me into a sitting position. He leaned down and kissed me. His lips carried my flavor, and I was accepting of the fact that nothing was going to be off limits for us. There was too much history between us to be embarrassed or shy about what went on in the bedroom…or in the office, as was this case. Plus, it was such a turn on to know that a man wanted you so badly that there wasn't anything that would stop him from having you.

Damien spent years making me feel weak, and in a matter of two weeks and one long overdue confession, he's managed to make me feel stronger than I ever have. He had always held all the power over me, and with three little words, he willingly handed over that power to me. I had a feeling before this weekend was over, I'd be saying them back to him.

"How am I supposed to work now after that?"

"That was the entire point."

"I'll be home as soon as I can, okay?"

Damien leaned down and kissed me again. "I'll see you soon, baby."

I didn't turn around as I heard him unlock the door and shut it behind him. I hopped off my desk very aware that I was panty-less, but as there was nothing that I could do about that now, I decided to get back to work and hopefully I could keep my focus long enough to actually get something done.

After working like a lunatic, I managed to get out of Fiona's in under a couple of hours. It was around four when I pulled in my driveway next to a black Mercedes. I felt so giddishly stupid at the joy of seeing his car parked next to mine.

What a turn of events. Who would have thought the boy who had brought me so much misery as a child would be the only man that I'd fall in love with years later?

I unlocked the front door, and throwing my purse on the couch, went in search of Damien. I found him in the second bedroom on his laptop working away. "Hey."

I was standing in the doorway of my makeshift office when he looked up. "I hope you don't mind me using your office to work."

I had to laugh. "It's not a problem to break into my house, but using my office without permission might be an issue? You are a strange one, Damien Greystone."

He leaned back in the chair and rested his hands over his ripped stomach. "I'm just making sure I never bore you."

I strode into the room. "Boredom is probably the only offense I can't lay at your feet."

He gave me a wicked grin. "I know something you can lay at my feet."

"Oh, and what's that?"

He leaned up and shot me a look full of sin. "Your knees as I fuck your delicious mouth."

God, how was it possible that I could go from loathing this man to craving his every threat in a matter of days? He was erasing the past with every touch, kiss, and mind-blowing orgasm.

I made my way to the chair, and before he could move, I straddled him knowing very well I was still naked beneath my skirt. The zipper of his slacks pressed against my core. Damien placed his hands on my hips and held me firm. "You need me to return earlier's favor?"

He studied my face before he answered. "Don't you know by now? Every time you let me touch you, it's *you* doing *me* the favor, baby. I don't deserve you, but that doesn't mean I'm not going to selfishly keep you."

Well, since we were being honest here. "C…can I tell you something?"

His brows drew inward. "Anything, Halloween."

"You have just as much power over me as you claim I have over you." I knew I might be making a mistake by telling him my secret. There would be nothing stopping him from abusing the power he now knew he had, but real love was done without fear. I had to trust him. Trust this. "I feel desperate when you're not around. I feel insecure and my body feels actual physical pain when I start missing your touch. I want you inside me all the time, Damien."

His face softened and I could actually see his emotions in those deep green depths of his. "Fiona, I do-"

"No. Please let me finish." He rolled his lips between his teeth, silencing himself. "I…" I averted my eyes for a second. This next part was hard and tricky. Looking back into his eyes, I found the nerve to finish. "I spend a lot of nights reliving our graduation night, h…how you took me so hard and deep. Some nights it felt as if I could still actually feel you inside me. But…but the feeling I remember most about that night…" God, he was going to think I was a freak. "I…when you…"

He took pity on me. "Baby, you can tell me anything. Don't ever be embarrassed with me. There is nothing you can tell me that will ease my need for you. Nothing will ever diminish the strength of my love you for. Nothing, Fiona."

Oh, God. I was so helpless when he said things like that to me.

"You felt so imposing when you held me down with your body, but when you covered my mouth with your hand, rendering me incapable of calling out for help if I needed it…it had me so turned on that I thought I was going to combust with it. It forced me to trust you. It forced me to accept that whatever you were going to do to me, you weren't going to hurt me while you did it. Even the pain from ripping me open felt glorious. I trusted you with every inch of my body, Damien, and I still do."

"Hopefully soon, you'll trust me with your love, too."

CHAPTER 20

Just when you think you can have it all…

Damien ~

After Fiona's confession yesterday, I had spent the entire night fucking her until she had begged for sleep. If she hadn't had to work this morning, I wouldn't have conceded. However, I had taken pity on her body and had finally let her fall asleep around ten.

Tonight, however, was going to be a different story. Knowing her kink was letting me call the shots had my mind on overdrive with all the things I wanted to do to her. I've already brought to life almost every fantasy I have ever had about her, except one. I'd been holding off until she was more comfortable with our relationship, but now…well, now I had every intention of holding her down and covering her screams with my hand as I slammed my cock into her hot, tight ass. I was going to pop her second cherry in the exact same manner that I popped her first, and I planned on making her love every second of it. And, so help me God, her ass better be cherry or there'd be no telling what I'd do.

I stayed up long after she had fallen asleep and wondered how I was going to make shit right with her. I still had one secret left that was weighing on me and I needed to find a way to make it right. That was how I found myself at her parents' house while she was at work.

Fiona was right about her parents. Her mother was weak, and her father was a classic addict. I knew I was shaking hands with a dangerous situation when I had approached her father, but like always, I did whatever I had to in order to be near her.

Fiona wasn't due home until noon, so as soon as I had deemed it a respectable hour, I had called her father and told him not to go into work this morning, and that I'd meet him at his place around ten. Two hours was plenty of time for me to finish shit up with her father and get back home. And now I stood in front of a man I wanted to beat stupid for putting his hands on what's mine.

"What do you mean I have to go to GA? That was never part of the deal. You never said I had to go to counseling. You said I could cash those checks with no issue. Now you're saying I have to stop gambling? That's bullshit!"

I shook my head. "I said you could cash some checks against your end-of-year bonuses. I never said you could write and cash unlimited blank checks, Jared."

"Exactly! You didn't, at any time, imply that there was going to be stipulations." I had a good five inches on the man, but Jared was standing tall against me, or rather against the threat to his gambling.

"You're lucky I'm just insisting that you go to gamblers anonymous instead of charging you with embezzlement after learning that you hit Fiona." I was doing my best to contain my anger, but rage kept simmering at the surface every time I thought about this man hitting my Fiona.

He had the balls to puff up at me. "Fiona is my daughter and what happens between us is none of your business."

"She may be your daughter, but that doesn't give you or *anyone* license to put their hands on a woman." I had to take a step back from this man before I started beating him in his own living room.

"Ha! I'm not as stupid as you'd to think I am, Greystone. We'd never had a relationship until you bought out Smith Tees. You didn't think I'd put it together when you approached me? The whole goddamn town knows who you are, where you went, and what you've accomplished. That's the price for being the town's prince, especially when you went after your father. That news spread like wildfire, my boy."

I stepped back into his personal space. "You don't know as much as you'd like to think-"

"I know you approaching me had something to do with Fiona. You guys went to school together, she is our only connection, and you can't deny it when I've seen that same black Mercedes parked outside in front of my house parked in her driveway, too."

"Fiona and I are none of your business, Jared. I came here as a courtesy. Yeah, I may have planned all this to get to Fiona, but that doesn't change-"

"What?"

The stunned question asked in a whisper had me turning my head so fast that heat rushed up my neck. Fiona was standing in the foyer of her parents' house. I'd been so caught up in not wanting to strangle her father that I hadn't heard her come in.

"What are you doing here, Fiona?" Jared asked. "You don't answer our calls and ignore your mother for weeks, and then just decide it's okay to-"

I turned to her father, ready to attack. "Keep speaking to her like that and I will do more than take everything you own. I will fucking *kill* you."

Jared blanched and wisely shut his mouth.

I looked back at Fiona and saw she wasn't even paying any attention to her father. "What's he talking about, Damien? What's going on?"

I wasn't going to have this conversation in front of her degenerate father. I wasn't going to give this man anything more that he could use against her. "Let's go home and I'll explain everything."

She glanced quickly at her father, and thank fuck, she didn't want to have this conversation in front of him any more than I did. She nodded. "I'll meet you there." She turned and walked right back out the front door without uttering a single word to her father.

I turned and left him with one last piece of advice before I followed Fiona home. "I will only say this once. You are going to get help for your gambling and you're going to start being the husband and father you should have always been. If not, I will do everything in my power to take everything you have from you. Believe me, don't believe, I really don't give a fuck. However, if I hear of you mistreating Fiona ever again, I will do more than ruin you. I will make you pray for death." I didn't wait for him to respond. I walked out of his house slamming the door behind me.

The drive to Fiona's was too long and too short. I was fucked, and I wasn't going into this thinking anything otherwise. I knew my only option was honesty, but the fear of losing her had my hands sweaty against the steering wheel. She had asked for one thing, and one thing only after everything I've done to her, and that had been to never lie to her. And while some people might argue that I hadn't technically lied to her, I knew she wouldn't see it that way. Hell, I didn't see it that way.

I pulled into her driveway and actually had to count to ten before I got out of my car. This was unfamiliar territory for me. I didn't do scared. I didn't do nervous. I didn't do anxious. But then there was never anything I ever really cared about, except her. Will was a close second, but even he knew that he was no match for Fiona.

The front door was unlocked, almost mocking me as it encouraged me to walk through to meet my demise. Since her house was so small, I walked right in on her pacing her living room. The second she heard me come in, she pounced. "What the fuck was all that about, Damien? Why were you at my parents' house? What did my father mean? What did *you* mean when you said you may have planned all of this? Planned what?!" Fiona was shrieking by the time she was done with her questions.

I could feel my blood turning to ice as I laid bare my final secret. "I bought Smithtown Textiles five years ago. Four years ago, I had upper management promote your father to the accounting department. Three years ago, I approached him and befriended him, allowing him to write check advancements against his yearly bonuses." The look on her face was one of nothing but torment, but I continued. "I knew he had a gambling problem. I've known it for years, even when we were kids. I made it a point to know *everything* about you and your family."

I knew she knew where I was going with this, but she demanded the words anyway. "Why?"

"I had always planned to come back for you. Always," I told her. "From the second I climbed out your window graduation night to the second I walked into your office with the intention of blackmailing you, I felt as if my life had been put on hold. These past ten years were just a means to an end for me. Everything I did, everything I accomplished, all that I've ever done was all to forage a path back to you."

"Damien-"

I held up my hand to stop her. I needed to get this all out. There was no way she would love me or be with me if there was even a hint of wrongdoing in our relationship. "I knew there was no way in hell I could come back here and simply ask you out. I knew you wouldn't give me the time of day unless I forced it, and I couldn't and wouldn't have blamed you. So, I set the wheels in motion five years ago to give you no choice but to have to accept me. I knew your dad wouldn't be able to help himself. The blank checks would be too tempting for an addict such as himself. So, I sat back for three years as I watched and waited for your dad to dig himself into a hole so deep that I'd have everything I need to force your hand."

Her face was covered in a flow of tears by the time I was done explaining the level of my duplicity. "Were you ever going to send my parents to prison? If I had said no, would you have gone through with it? Would you have pressed charges?"

I knew my answer was going to damn me, but I couldn't lie to her. "Yes."

She let out an anguish sob as she wrapped her arms around her waist. "You would have sent them to prison for taking the bait you set up for them?"

"Yes. If I couldn't have you, then I was going to make sure I wasn't the only one who was going to be miserable for the rest of their life. I had every intention of taking you down with me. I wasn't going to settle for anything less than having you, Fiona, and if that wasn't going to happen, well, then I wasn't going to allow you to be happy without me."

Her eyes flashed and the rage on her face was unmistakable. "Who the fuck do you think you are? What makes you think you can just *play* with people's lives? Are you so selfish and so evil that it doesn't play on your conscience at all to destroy people's happiness just for the sake of winning?"

I couldn't help the beast arousing inside me. She did that to me. Only her. "It doesn't when the prize of winning is *you.*"

That only seemed to inflame her fury. "I'm not some goddamn prize!"

I stormed over to her, then grabbing her by her arm and yanking her towards me, locking her to my body, I stared down at her fuming and unguarded. "No, you're not. But you seem to still be unaware of exactly what you mean to me, Fiona. You seem to think that when I say I'm obsessed with you that I'm exaggerating or throwing out common phrases that all couples use. Well, here's the complete truth. When I say I love you, I don't mean I love you in the traditional sense, I mean I love you like I can't *fucking breathe* with it. When I say I'm obsessed with you, I don't mean I'm addicted to your body and I just want to fuck you. I mean that every thought, every action, and every emotion I have ever felt since I was five revolves around *you.* And when I say I will kill any man who touches you, *I mean just that.*"

She wasn't hearing me. "You say you love me but all you do is manipulate and hurt me. How can you say you love me but lie and torment me? You don't love me, Damien. You love the power that you feel making another human being cave to you. You love the power that you feel knowing you can play God with people's lives…with *my* life."

I threw my head back and the laugh I let out was as sinister as it got. "I play God every day at work, Fiona. I hold people's financial futures in my hands. People cave to me all day, every day." I got right into her face. "And none of it makes me feel a fucking thing. No one or nothing makes me feel anything, except for *you.* The only time I feel powerful is when I think of you, are seeing you, and Sweet Jesus, when I'm inside of you." I shook her body, hoping it would make her finally understand the depths of my sickness. "And you're right, I *love* the way it feels when you make me feel invincible, and I'm not giving that feeling up for anything in the world!"

Fiona gasped, and wrenching her arm out of my grasped, stepped back from me. "You're going to have to find a way to give it up because I want nothing more to do with you! Get the fuck out of my house!" She closed her eyes and really started sobbing.

I stuck my hands in my pockets to keep the beast from dragging her into the bedroom and not giving her a choice. My voice was quiet and lethal. "Look at me, Fiona." She raised her sorrowful brown gaze to mine. "Do you really believe I'm going to walk out of this house and never come back?"

She was stunning in her rage. Fiona's innocent always glowed, and her submission was powerful. But after all the years she spent cowering underneath my bullying, Fiona was magnificent when she showed her strength. She was and always has been the most beautiful thing I've ever seen. "I'll call the police then. I'll get a restraining order against you. Just like you can excuse everything you've done by convincing yourself it was a necessity, I can do the same."

I took a step towards her, and she did the one thing she shouldn't have.

She ran.

She ran towards her bedroom and I followed. Men were primal creatures, and me, maybe more than most. So, when she ran, there was no way the animal in me wasn't going to chase her. I was on her heels, so she didn't have enough time to shut and lock the door before I was slamming it open after her.

Her eyes widened, and she stepped back. *"I said, get out of my house!"*

I kept going until her back hit the wall and I cowered her until she didn't have a choice but to look up at me. I wrapped a fistful of her brown silk in my hands and held her still while I brought my other hand up and pinned her against the wall by her throat. "I'm going to leave *only* to give you time to calm down, but I will be back, Fiona. If you think I'm going to live the rest of my life without you, especially now that I've had you, you're out of your goddamn mind."

She didn't back down, even when I squeezed her neck for emphasis. "I'll call the police if I have to, Damien. Don't think I won't."

I just nodded at her threat. "Good, because you're going to have to in order to keep me away from you, Halloween."

Her eyes widened as they became glassy. "You can't-"

"Make no mistake, Fiona. Prison is the *only* thing that will keep me away from you." I let go of her, and grabbing my laptop, left her crying in the bedroom. I didn't bother with my clothes or toiletries because I was going to be back, even if it was just to be sent to prison.

CHAPTER 21

No one heals from this kind of pain…no one.

Fiona ~

I spent all day Saturday alternating between crying and raging. I had called Vicky first thing when I had woken up, and she had spent the day with me supporting whichever mood swing was front and center at the time. She hadn't judged, and she hadn't offered any kind of advice. Being my best friend for so many years, she knew there weren't any words to ease the impact to my life that was Damien Greystone.

When I had left work earlier than I had intended on Friday, I thought life was perfect as I'd been driving across town to pick up dinner. I'd had plans of being too spent to cook. The dread that consumed me had been overwhelming when I had spotted Damien's car in front of my parents' house. I never dreamed my world would come crashing down around me hours later.

I had cried myself to sleep again last night and had woken up this morning feeling worse if that was even possible. I had come to realize that it wasn't necessarily what Damien had done that had broken my heart; it was the fact that I had finally reached a point where I trusted him, and I'd been blindsided once again by his games. I mean, c'mon, reflecting back on all the things he's ever done to me, manipulating my father was one of the least of his offenses. I just thought that part of our relationship was over, and it hurt to find out that it hadn't been.

A part of me also wondered if I was just being a coward again. His intensity was intimidating, and I wondered if I was strong enough to be the recipient of such emotion. A sudden knock at the door brought me out of my musings.

I expected to see Vicky on the other side of the threshold, but instead, I opened the door to a sweet-looking Jason, and the sight of him felt like a sledgehammer to my gut. "Jason…"

His face brightened with a sheepish smile. "Hey, Fee."

I stood there in shock and it wasn't until he asked if he could come in that my female vanity made an appearance. I was mortified by how awful I must look. I'd been crying for two days. I knew I looked a hot mess while he looked perfect with his blonde hair and blue eyes, looking all wholesome and sweet.

I stepped back and pulled the door open wider. "Yeah, uh...sure."

I foolishly ran my fingers through my hair and tried to push my puffy eyes in, but I knew nothing short of a miracle was going to undo the damage. It was past noon, and I was still dressed in a tank top and pajama bottoms. I just needed to start my period to make this weekend of humiliation complete.

"Uh, I know this is kind of unexpected, but…you wouldn't return any of my calls or respond to my texts, and even if you do have a new boyfriend, we were friends way before anything else had happened. I was kind of hoping we could still be friends, Fiona. I miss you, and believe it or not, I miss Vicky, too." He let out a small laugh and I had never felt so bad.

"Jason, I never got any texts or calls from you. Af….after, uh, that phone call, I thought you must just be mad at me." I shrugged. "Which I didn't blame you if you had been."

He cocked his head at me. "Where's your phone?"

I went to my bedroom to retrieve my phone. Walking back into the living room, I saw Jason with his phone out. "I'm calling you."

I looked down at my phone and there was nothing. I started getting a sinking feeling in my stomach when he said he just sent me a text and, again, nothing.

"My number's been blocked, Fiona."

I closed my eyes at the realization. When I opened them back up, Jason was looking at me with a small smile playing on his lips. "I take it you didn't block me?"

I shook my head. "I would never do that, Jason. Like you said, we were friends way before anything else came into play."

He took my phone out of my hand, and after tapping away for a bit, he called me again from his phone, and this time, it rang. I looked up at him. "I'm so sorry, Jason."

"It's okay, Fio-"

I shook my head. "No, it's not. You don't deserve to be dragged into my drama. I don't know why he'd do something so ridic-"

"I do."

My breath stopped when Jason stepped towards me. He was standing so close that I had to tilt my head back to look at him. He wasn't as tall or as wide as Damien, but he was still bigger than I was. "You forget, Fiona. I've had you. And speaking as a man who has seen you give into your pleasure, I don't blame the man one bit. I'd do the same. Hell, most men worth their salt would."

My face flushed at his personal compliment and reminder of our time together. "I think it's because you're the only other man I've ever been with-"

Jason threw his head back and laughed. "Now it makes even more sense."

"What does?" I asked, confused.

He brought his hand up and caressed my face. "Awe, Fee. In a perfect world we would only ever know one lover. We'd all be virgins until our wedding nights and only share that experience with the one person we're meant for. But we don't live in a perfect world and, sweetheart, I have to say, I'm feeling pretty proud of myself that I'm the only other man you've been with. And while I'm feeling proud, he's feeling threatened just like any other man would."

"That sounds ridiculous and cavemanish, Jason."

He pulled his hand from my face and gifted me with one of his signature smiles. "It's both, but that doesn't make it any less true. Just like you have to be a woman to understand that time of the month or pregnancy, you have to be a man to understand our level of possessiveness and need to conquer."

He sounded just like Damien, just a more watered-down version.

"So, we're to feel flattered instead of frustrated?"

He outright laughed. "Nah, sweetheart. If it's not making you feel desired, then it's being done wrong. Do you feel desired?"

His question brought back a rush of memories and images of Damien driving into me and I could feel my face flush with heat. Yeah, I felt desired among other things.

Jason read my reaction perfectly. "Seems to me like he's doing everything right."

"If you think manipulation and lying are the right things to do, then I guess."

"Fiona, it only seems that way if you're a woman. If you're a man, it falls under protectiveness and need." Before I could respond to his absurd man-logic, there came another knock at the door.

His brows rose. "Did my coming here interrupt something?"

I headed towards the door. "No. It's most likely Vicky."

I opened the door for a second time today, and this time, it was Vicky on the other side. "Damn, Fee, you look like shit."

I snorted as I stepped back to let her in. "Gee, thanks." I shut the door. "Just so you know, I was already very aware of my appearance. No need to broadcast it."

Vicky stood shock-still in my living room. No doubt, Jason's presence had her befuddled. She looked back at me. "Uh, am I interrupting something?"

"Hey, Vee," Jason said as he walked over and gave her a hug. "I was just telling Fiona that I missed hanging out with you two weirdos."

Vicky shot me a look of complete what-the-hell. She looked back at Jason after I gave her a noncommittal shrug. "It's good to see you too, Jase. I just kind of didn't expect to see you around, considering all that went down with Fee's new boyfriend." Vicky *never* avoided the elephant in the room.

"Yeah, I figured." He jerked his head towards me. "From the little that she's told me, he doesn't seem like the sharing type."

Vicky snorted. "He's a psychopath. It's a miracle he allows *me* to spend time with her."

Jason raised his brows at me. "A psychopath?"

I nodded because, really, what else could I do. It was true. Damien was an absolute undiagnosed psychopath.

A psychopath who made my body sing with pleasure and my heart weep in agony.

"Okay, I may be taking my life in my own hands here, but how about you take a shower and I take you girls to a late lunch?" Jason suggested.

"Fuck that, Jase. Fiona's heartbroken if you can't tell by the puffy eyes, wrinkled ensemble, and rat's nest on top of her head." Vicky plopped herself down on the couch. "We need this to be an early dinner that comes with alcohol and bad decisions." She shook her head. "Lunch just ain't going to cut it."

Jason laughed. "Okay. I can do an early dinner with drinks and bad decisions." Then he eyed her. "How bad are we talking about?"

"Bad like, I-want-to-wake-up-possibly-impregnated-by-a-total-stranger bad."

I let out my first genuine laugh since Friday. God, I loved this woman, and if she ends up pregnant by a complete stranger, I have every intention of helping her raised that sweet baby. But then a thought occurred to me. "You don't think that'd ruin things between you and Will?"

She huffed. "Puhlease, unless his dick can reach me all the way from New York, my legs ain't staying closed for a man who I know isn't keeping his pants on for me."

"Okay, who's Will?"

"Okay, while I go jump in the shower and try to make myself presentable, Vicky can tell you all about her new friend, William Creston."

I scurried on into my bedroom and gathered my clothes before heading to the bathroom to shower. As I made me way over, I could hear Vicky telling Jason all about Will. I turned on the shower, and stepping underneath the spray, I had to admit it felt wonderful. I knew I couldn't hold a pity party forever and tonight was the first step to getting my shit together.

As I showered, my thoughts wandered to Jason. I thought it was weird that I could hang out with him and feel nothing sexual when I had just slept with him not too long ago. When I tried to think back to the sex, it was like a distant memory that carried no emotion. Earlier when he touched my face, my first thought had been that he shouldn't be touching me because of Damien. I had felt nothing other than trepidation that he was overstepping when I belonged to another man.

But I didn't belong to another man. I had kicked that other man out of my house and had told him not to come back. Yet here I was, in the shower, confused and angry about it.

I finished showering but stayed under the cold spray as long as I could to try to diminish my puffy eyes. When I couldn't take the cold anymore, I got out and proceeded to get ready. Since my mission was to just get drunk and not get impregnated by a stranger, I kept with the basics. A little mascara, a touch of lip gloss, my hair thrown up in a messy bun, and then I was ready to go in my green summer dress. I just needed to strap on my sandals, and we could go.

I went and grabbed my shoes from my bedroom, then made my way into the living room. I sat down on one of the mismatched armchairs. "Have you guys decided where we should go?"

Jason was sitting on the couch next to Vicky with his arm draped over the backrest. "Nope. Vicky just finished filling me in on her night of cucumber debauchery, so we haven't gotten that far yet."

"I'm not picky. I just need enough food to offset the liquor, so that I don't fall out before midnight."

Jason leaned up a little. "Midnight? You do know that it's only a little past three, Fiona, right? You're talking almost ten hours of drinking."

I held up a finger. "That is an incorrect assessment, sir. By the time we get to wherever we choose to eat, it'll be closer to four. Then we'll order and bullshit, which will kill at least an hour, if not an hour and a half, bringing us upon the six o'clock hour or so. Then we'll make our way to the bar of our choosing, which will most likely be Mercury's, and that will kill another fifteen minutes or so. By the time we find a table and order our first round, we'll be closer to seven giving us a window of four or five hours to drink since we all have to work in the morning."

Jason clapped. "My apologies. I defer to the professionals."

I started laughing at his nonsense. "Seriously, unless we all plan on calling in sick tomorrow, I think we're going to have to hold off on getting pregnant until next weekend."

"Way to kill my dreams, Fee. What have I ever done to you to deserve that?"

"You can thank me nine months from now when you're not delivering a kid, thus ruining all your future tequila-riddled nights."

"She's got a point," Jason agreed.

Vicky chewed on her lower lip. "Maybe."

"Okay, finishing putting your shoes on, Fiona, and-" Another knock on the door clouded the room in silence.

"Jesus, is this Visit Fiona Day?" I mumbled. With my luck, it was probably my parents wanting me to save them from another disastrous situation they've put themselves in. I headed towards the door barefooted.

Jason and Vicky stood up simultaneously. "Fiona, hold up a sec…" Vicky started.

I had my hand on the doorknob as I looked back. "Why? What's up?"

I could see her and Jason exchange uneasy glances. "What if it's Damien?

Fee, he'll lose his shit if he sees Jason here."

I let out a hopeless huff. "Damien is not going to drive down here on a Sunday, Vicky. Besides, he's Damien Greystone III. I'm sure he's knee-deep in females willing to help him forget all about me."

I twisted the knob and pulled the door open. My heart leapt into my throat as my eyes took in the fact that it was, indeed, Damien standing at my front door. "Damien, what-"

He pushed his way in and stormed into the living room. I shut the door as his eyes made their way to Jason. He turned around and the look on his face had me wanting to run.

CHAPTER 22

Prison it is.

Damien ~

People say 'I just saw red' or 'I blanked out' all the time and you think it's just an expression. Well, I'm here to tell you that it's not. Because the second I saw that sonofabitch, Jason, standing in Fiona's living room, I lost my goddamn mind.

There were too many things attacking me at once as he stood there assessing me. This was the only other man who has ever touched Fiona in a way that was my right only. This man has kissed her body and knows what it feels like to be inside her. And now this same man was standing in her living room only days after she tells me to leave and never come back.

If I was going to prison, then it was going to be worth it all the way around. I charged him and-smart man-he saw it coming. However, he wasn't quick enough to avoid the blow. I hit that fucker as if I had just caught him in bed with Fiona.

"Damien!" Fiona screamed.

Jason fought back, and it just fueled my need to destroy him. I could hear the girls screaming and pleading with us to stop, but they'd have better luck trying to unlock two rams fighting for dominance.

Every sound was a vague orchestra to our punches. The furniture breaking, the girls' endless pleas, the grunts, none of it could break through the blood rushing through my ears.

Fiona was fucking mine whether she wanted to be or not. And I meant what I said when I told her I'd kill any man who touched her. I didn't know what he was doing here, and I didn't give a fuck. All I knew was that he was too close to Fiona for my liking.

He wasn't a pussy, I could say that for him. Unfortunately for him, I had obsessive rage on my side. I hit the fucker until I saw blood squirt from his face, then worked my fury on his body. He hit back and even landed a few, but it did nothing to deter me.

"Damien! Stop! Please, stop!" Fiona begged.

I wasn't going to stop. I was going to keep hitting him until he was dead. However, my plan ended abruptly when Vicky jumped in between us. I wasn't my father, and no matter how enraged I may be, I'd never hit a woman. *Ever.*

As soon as I pulled my fist back, Fiona was wrapping her arms around my waist trying to pull me back. *"Damien, stop! Oh, God! Please, stop!"*

I turned my back on Jason and stared Fiona down. *"Two days?* My side of the fucking bed isn't even cold yet, and you bring this motherfucker into our home?"

I didn't care that it was technically her house. *She* was my home. Therefore, anywhere she was at, that was *my fucking home.*

I noticed her hands were balled into fists at her side. "It's not like that! We're friends!"

"No, you are not! You're out of your ever-lovin' mind if you think I will allow you to be friends with someone you used to fuck!"

"That's bullshit!" I whirled around as Vicky found her voice. "They were friends way before anything ever happened between them, and unless you're going to stand there and tell us you've kept your dick in your pants for the past ten years, then you and your dictations can go to hell!"

I knew Fiona was going to hate me, but I didn't care right now. Nothing else mattered in this moment, except getting Jason away from Fiona. I stalked towards Vicky-and credit to Jason as he stepped up next to her-held nothing back. "Test me, Victoria." My voice had never been so controlled and so cold. "Test me on this and see what happens. You above anyone else on earth should know what lengths I'll go to for her. I'm not scared to go to prison, and I'm not scared to go to prison for murder. So, make your *fucking move!"*

Fiona was in between us in a flash. *"Damien, please!"*

I looked down at the only person who could drive me to the brink of madness. "Get rid of them both or, so help me God, I will burn this fucking place to the ground with both of them in it!"

Jason stepped up, and I didn't know whether to praise his bravery or mock his stupidity. His face was bloody, and I noted that he didn't wipe it away. "We'll leave." He grabbed Vicky's hand, and I saw him squeeze the shit out of it. "We're leaving, but if anything happens to Fiona or Vicky, you're going to have to kill me because I *will* come after you. They're my friends whether you like it or not."

I stepped to him because this *was* a battle for dominance, even if he was the one covered in blood and not me. "Fiona and Vicky aren't yours to protect. Fiona is *mine.* Fiona has *always been mine.* You may have been lucky enough to experience her, but she was never going to be yours. *Never."*

"I'm not here to bump dicks with you. Even if you keep Fiona away from me, Vicky is still my friend," he countered.

I laughed at that and looked over at Vicky. "We'll see what Will has to say about that, won't we?"

Vicky looked ready to do battle, but before she could attack, Fiona jumped in. "Please, just please, stop!" She stood in front of me looking at her friends. "It's fine, guys. I…I'll be okay. It'll be okay. I'll call you. I promise."

Vicky begrudgingly tugged on Jason's arm and pulled him behind her as they left. As soon as I heard the door shut, I grabbed Fiona by the arm and swung her around to face me. "I'm only going to say this once, Fiona. If you don't want your boyfriend six feet under then stay the fuck away from him!"

She tried to break my hold, but there was no way I was letting go of her. "He's not my boyfriend. I'm not a whore, Damien, no matter what I let you do to me in the bedroom," she seethed.

I grabbed her other arm and yanked her forward until her body was flushed with mine. "If you think the things that I've done to you so far qualify you as a whore, the things I still have planned for you are sure to make you feel like a filthy slut. Anything you let Jason do to you is going to be like chaste kisses compared to the depraved things I'm going to make you *fucking love.*" Fiona freed her arm and slapped me so hard that my face snapped sideways.

And my dick got rock hard.

Deep down, I knew she hadn't been with Jason, but that didn't ease the need to claim her again. I gathered as much of her hair as I could in my hand and drug her towards the bedroom. Had she asked me to stop, I would have. Had she started crying and pleading with me to let her go, I would have. Not because I would walk away, but because she wasn't the violent type and for her to slap me, I knew she had reached her limit.

But she didn't do or say anything. Fiona *let* me lead her to the bedroom and that gave me all the permission I needed to ruin her for all other men.

Once I got her in the bedroom, I threw her up against the wall and slammed my mouth down on hers. I told myself that if she didn't open her mouth up for me, I'd leave and give her more time to calm down. But if…if she did open those sweet lips for me, nothing would stop me from ripping her apart.

I slanted my lips over hers and just when I thought she was slipping through my fingers, Fiona let out a tortured moan and opened for me. I slipped my tongue inside her hot, waiting mouth and kissed her like I was tongue fucking her pussy. A normal man couldn't handle my need for this woman. She might kick me out when this was all over, but I would own her body until she suffered withdrawals from the pleasure that only *I* could give her.

Fiona ran her hands up my arms and buried them in my hair, anchoring me to her mouth. The second she did so, I ran the hand that wasn't tangled in her hair up her leg, thanking every deity out there that she had on a dress, and ripped her panties clean off her body.

I had to release my hold on her hair as I took both her thighs in my hands and lifted her, so that her pussy cradled my cock as she wrapped her legs around my waist. I press my steel against her core, and she tore her lips away from mine to let out a desperate gasp. "Oh, God…"

"Even He can't save you from me, baby." If she thought the marks that I left on her before were over the top, by the time I was done with her, she was going to look like she'd been beaten. I bit my way down her neck, and instead of going with the cutesy nibble, I bit down on her neck until her blood coated my tongue.

"Damien!"

I held her to the wall with my body, and with my teeth still latched onto her neck, I used my hands to unbutton my jeans and lower my shit far enough to get my dick out. Supporting her thighs in my hands again and spreading them as far as I could, I slammed my cock into pussy. Luckily for her, she was so wet that I was able to enter her with minimal resistance.

I pulled back from her neck and the vicious mark left on her had me growling like a fucking animal. I pumped into her cunt with so much force that her body was climbing up the wall. I slipped out, and after a pump so potent that it pushed her up several inches, I was done with the wall.

I carried her over to the bed, and dropping her on it, I grabbed her by her hips and flipped her over. I hurriedly threw off my shirt and removed the rest of my clothes. I climbed up on the bed behind her and her flimsy dress was no match for my need for her. I reached over, and grabbing both straps, I ripped that shit down the middle until it fell flat underneath her on the bed. I removed her bra, and then she was perfectly naked, bent over in front of me.

I ran my hand up her back until it settled on the back of her neck. Then I circled my fingers around her and pushed down until I was certain she couldn't fight me. I leaned over and covered her body with mine as I whispered in her ear, "Tell me you want my cock, baby."

She whimpered but didn't say anything as I licked the back of her shoulder.

I rubbed my cock up and down her wet slit. *"Fucking* tell me."

"Damien, please…don't tease me…"

"Well, since you don't want to tell me how to please you, I'll just have to figure it out for myself." I buried myself inside her wet cunt until my pelvis was flushed with her ass. I felt the tip of my dick knock up against the wall of her cervix, and she let out a brutal cry.

Slamming into her pussy, I slipped the fingers on my free hand inside her along with my dick. I needed her cream, but I wasn't going to take my cock out to get it. She took in a ragged breath when I took my cream-soaked fingers and traced that forbidden puckered hole of hers. Her reaction confirmed my hope that she'd never been touched there and all I knew was that if she let me in, I'd never believe her again if she told me that she wanted me gone. No woman gave up that part of her body unless she was in love or an outright whore.

And Fiona was no whore.

It wasn't hard to slip a finger inside as covered as my fingers were in her wetness. I leaned over her stiff body, whispering in her ear, "Breathe, baby. I need you to breathe for me." I wanted to ruin her, but I didn't want to do untold damage to her body. I planned on fucking her in the ass a million times over by the time we were dead, so I needed to make this pleasurable for her.

"Damien, I…"

"Shh, baby, just relax. I promise to make you love it, Halloween."

I could feel her body relax against my invasion, and after a few strokes, I slid another finger into her tight ass. I matched the strokes to the thrusting of my cock, then slowly but surely, I could feel her give into the sensations. "You like that, baby?"

"Yes." It was barely audible, but I heard her, nonetheless.

I straightened up and leaned back as far as I could and watched both my cock and my fingers breach her fuckholes, and I had never seen a dirtier, sexier, hungrier sight in all my life. It was a miracle I wasn't blowing my load yet.

I was so enraptured by the sight of her body that I missed what she was saying. I removed my hand from the back of her neck and used it to lift her chin off the bed. "What's that baby?"

"Do it."

My heart started beating with enough force to push out of my chest. "Do what, Fiona?"

"Do it…like…like…"

I knew what she wanted, but I needed to hear her say it. I needed permission. "What, baby? You have to tell me what you want. Tell me how you need it. Tell me how you need *me* to give it to you."

She let out a deep moan as I scissored my fingers in her ass, opening her up wider. My dick was too thick not to hurt her, but I was going to do my best. "Graduation night, Damien. Take me like graduation night."

I ran my hand from her chin and covered her mouth airtight with it, then taking my fingers out of her ass, I took a hold of my cock and guided the head to the opening of her forbidden entrance. My cock was drenched in her juices, and because it was so fucking hard, I was able to slam my way into her tight, hot ass in one thrust.

Fiona let out a scream that rivaled the one she had gifted me with when I had broken through her virginity ten years ago. Her fingers were clawing at the sheets and just when I thought I might have gone too far, she pushed her ass back to take me in even deeper.

I couldn't remember much after that, seeing as how I lost my damn mind with that one little movement. All I knew was that I never removed my hand from her mouth, and I rammed my cock into her ass with so much force and need that I didn't even notice when Fiona had bitten the palm of my hand.

I didn't stop until I felt her channel start to tremble around my cock. I held onto her hip with my other hand and knowing that she was cumming from my cock in her ass alone had me exploding inside her as I called out her name.

Minutes later-or hours, wasn't sure which-I pulled out of her body, and falling to my side, I gathered her up against me and just held her. Our heavy breathing was the only thing that could be heard.

After a few minutes, she whispered the one thing that gave me hope. "Was I the only virgin in this room tonight?"

I kissed the back of her neck. "No, baby, you weren't. That always belonged to you, too."

CHAPTER 23

I've got to be the stupidest person on the planet hands-down.

Fiona ~

There was stupid and then there was me.

I didn't think there was a word in the English language that could accurately describe the level of stupidity that I have engaged in and continued to engage in.

Instead of kicking Damien out of my house after he fought Jason, I let him use my body however he saw fit until I had fallen asleep from exhaustion.

And I had loved every second of it.

Getting ready for work this morning, the soreness I felt had me so turned on that I actually contemplated having Debbie cover for me, so I could drive to G&C and let him do it to me all over again.

I must be sick to crave the things he does to me.

I knew without a doubt that I was in love with Damien, but that knowledge did nothing but make me feel weak and stupid. Love was supposed to make you feel strong and secure, not helpless and confused. He's spent most his life hurting me, and loving him felt like a betrayal, a betrayal to my parents, to Jason, and even to Vicky. She, too, suffered by just being my best friend for all these years.

But it was those small gestures of affection; the quiet whispers of love, the way he made me feel when he was inside me, those small things that made me want to forgive him everything.

My *thoughts* made me feel like a fool while *he* made me feel loved.

I just didn't know how to not feel like a fool. I wanted a guarantee that if I gave myself to him completely, he'd never hurt me or my family and friends again. However, you couldn't get that kind of guarantee from a lunatic because *they're freakin' lunatics.*

I was two sane ideas away from dragging Vicky to a goddamn psychic and letting a complete stranger tell me which path to choose. That's how lost I felt.

Not even to mention, what would happen even if I did go for it? Would we live here or in San Francisco? Would I need to give up Fiona's or would he suffer the three-hour commute every day?

Fuck, I was not equipped to make all these grownup decisions.

I picked up the phone and dialed Vicky. It was either her and Mercury's, or Stella The Psychic-and yes, I actually looked one up.

She answered on the first ring, probably because she knew I was surfing the psychic network. "What up, nut?"

"I'm going crazy, Vee. Like *really* crazy. Not just being-part-of-the-band-so-we-can-get-in-free crazy."

"Hey! That was not crazy, that was ingenious," she objected.

"Yeah, up until the point where you told them you could fill in for the drummer." I'll never forget that night. I think we're still banned from that club.

"How the hell was I supposed to know there was a drum solo in that song?"

"Gee, I don't know. Maybe the fact that they were a *rock* group."

She harrumphed, clearly offended. "That didn't stop fans from asking for my autograph."

I started rubbing my temple. "You mean, Drunk Herb?"

"Did you just call me to ruin a beautiful memory?"

"No. I need drinks and some serious advice. No bullshit, Vee."

"I'll meet you at Mercury's in ten."

She hung up, and I fell in love with her just a little more. I'd rather have one loyal friend than fifty simple bitches that weren't really real. One Vicky was worth a thousand weak bitches. I gathered my stuff together and locked up my office.

To my surprise, Debbie stopped me on my way out. "Hey, Fiona, you got a sec?"

"Sure, what's up?"

She was biting her lower lip. "Uh, I really don't know how to say this without sounding…"

I waved away her concern. "Just tell me, Dee."

She took a deep breath. "You look like shit, Fee. And I'm not talking your normal morning-after with Vicky. I'm talking like I almost left a suicide hotline flyer on your desk earlier when you went to lunch."

I started laughing and I couldn't stop.

Debbie pointed at me. "See. That right there is disturbing, Fiona."

I got myself under control, but I couldn't help the little laughs that escaped. "I'm fine, honest."

"Do me a favor? Take tomorrow off. And if you need Wednesday, take that, too. Just to give me peace of mind, please," she begged.

Her face was nothing but sincere as I regarded her. "I don't deserve you, Debbie."

"True, but you're still the best boss I've ever had and if you go insane, I'd have to find another job and I just can't have that kind of disruption in my life right now. So, I'll see you Thursday, okay?"

I gave her a hug. "Okay."

I made it to Mercury's just in time to see Vicky getting out of her car. She made her way over towards me, and without a word, linking her arm around mine, we went into Mercury's on our mission.

I let Vicky steer me towards a back table. "No bar?"

"Nope, I have to go into the office tomorrow and if we sit at the bar, that's not going to happen." And as serious as she could be, she finished with, "I don't lie to myself, Fee."

I just laughed. "A table it is, then."

We sat down and one of the cocktail waitresses made her way over to us. "Your usual, ladies?"

Vicky winked at her. "You know it, Steph." When Stephanie walked away to go get our drinks, Vicky asked, "Okay, what gives, chick?"

I threw my head down on the table. "I want to forgive him, marry him, and have fifty little black-haired, green-eyed babies with him, Vee."

"Okaaay…"

I felt the table bounce a little when Stephanie set our customary bucket of beer down. I didn't lift my head until I heard Vicky crack open a beer. "I need your honest opinion, Vee, no matter how brutal."

She took a long swallow of her beer before she spoke. "There are only two options to choose from, Fiona."

"I know." Her statement wasn't helping me at all. "Choosing him makes me feel weak, though." I reached for a beer. "How can I love him after all he's done to me?" She tilted her head at me and that's when I realized it was the first time that I've ever said the words out loud to anyone.

"Fiona, I know he's done some horrible things to you and I know he's left you with some pretty deep scars, but…"

I took a drink of my beer because it felt like I was going to need it. "But what?"

"Everything that man has done, both good and bad, has been to find a way to hold onto you, Fiona. His lies and manipulations have all been to be with you. Yeah, his execution and methods run along the side of crazy and unhealthy, but because he's unbalanced, that man is going to love you for the rest of his life. Fiona, Damien loves you to distraction. He's going to spend all of his days finding new ways and, let's be honest, insane ways to cherish and worship you. I know without a doubt that he will never look at another woman as long as he has your love. Hell, he may not even look without your love."

I couldn't stop the tears from flowing. "Vicky…"

She reached over and placed her hands over mine. "He's offering you a love that most people can only dream about. He's going to make mistakes, and Lord knows that he's going to piss you off from every now and again, but that comes with all relationships."

"So, you're saying I should choose him?"

"I'm saying you should do what makes you happy. And, Fiona, when he's not fighting to find a way to tie you to him forever, he's making you happy. There is no other man on this earth who is going to love you like Damien does. He *wants* to be able to tell his grandchildren that he's loved their grandmother since he was five."

I couldn't stop the sobs if I had tried. I immediately felt Vicky's arms around me. "Fee, quit being scared of what he might do and accept that if he finally has you like he wants you, that man will never hurt you again."

I looked up. "How can you know this, but I don't?"

"Even Jason could see it, Fiona. Why do you think he took that ass whoopin' without calling the cops? When I got him home and cleaned him up, all he could talk about was that he'd never seen love in tangible form like that before and he even commented on how amazing it was to see," she answered.

As soon as Vicky resumed sitting in her seat, a box of tissue was dropped in the center of the table. Stephanie was so going to get a huge tip. "So, just forgive him everything and hand over my soul?"

She shrugged a shoulder. "Seems only fair since he sold his to the devil years ago just to be with you."

"I love you, Vee."

"I know you do." She signaled for Stephanie. "Now get your ass to San Fran and put the poor fool out of his misery before he ends up on the six o'clock news."

I jumped up, hugged her, then ran out of Mercury's.

I sat in traffic for what seemed like days. It humbled me to know that Damien has made this drive for me a few times and I knew he'd continue to if I asked him.

I wasn't going to lie and say I wasn't petrified. It was hard enough to trust someone completely who's never hurt you, but to take that leap of faith with someone who has a history of doing nothing *but* hurting you…well, that was some scary shit. *Love* was some scary shit.

The commute traffic gave me plenty of time to digest Vicky's words. She hadn't pointed out anything that he hadn't already confessed to me, but I knew now that I just didn't want to get my hopes up. She was right. The way he went about dealing with his feelings for me was wrong, but I couldn't deny the idea that he's loved me since we were five was the shit fairy tales were made out of.

I didn't want to pass that up just because I was scared. I'd been scared enough. I wanted to be brave and that included being brave enough to handle heartbreak if it came down to that. People who loved unguardedly, even after they've had their hearts broken, were the epitome of brave.

My biggest fear was that I would confess my love for him, and then he'd laugh in my face with a victorious 'checkmate' booming through his laughter. Still, I realized that I loved him, no matter what his reaction would be. Whether his love for me was real or not, it didn't change how I felt about him, so why hide it? Why hold on to it like a dirty secret?

I finally found myself on the streets of San Francisco heading towards G&C. The closer I got, the more nervous I became. I have been unsure of my feelings for this man all my life, and now that I was certain of what I felt, I had no idea how to tell him. I had no idea what kind of relationship we'd have now, but I knew I wanted to find out.

I was no longer eighteen, and I was no longer lost.

When I easily found a parking space near the building, I looked at the time on my phone and saw that it was almost seven already. I didn't even know if he was still at his office. But no matter, I'd track him down at his penthouse if I had to. Now that I've chosen him, I was going to see this through.

I sped-walked to the lobby's front doors, only to find them locked. I started pushing and pulling on them as if that would make them magically open. I could see a security guard making his way over to the doors. He didn't open them, but I could hear him clearly through the glass. "Office hours are closed."

"I know, but I need to see Damien…uh, Mr. Greystone."

"Then make an appointment during the appropriate hours, ma'am." He pointed to the watch on his wrist for emphasis.

"Please…I…I want to surprise him."

He finally took pity on me and opened the doors. "Surprise him? Are you some sort of strip-o-gram or something?"

I couldn't hold back my laugh. "I don't have that kind of confidence, sir." He smiled good-naturedly at me, so that gave me some hope. "My name's Fiona Eldstead and-"

"I'm sorry, what did you say your name was?"

"Fiona Eldstead."

He immediately pulled the door open and ushered me inside. After shutting the doors and re-locking them he turned towards me. "I'm so sorry Ms. Eldstead-"

"Please, call me Fiona."

He offered me a grateful smile. "I'm sorry, Fiona. Of course, business hours don't apply to you."

I knew my face looked as confused as I felt. "They don't?"

"No, ma'am. You're on Mr. Greystone's personal approval list."

My eyebrows shot up. "I am?"

"Yes, ma'am."

I peered at his name tag. "Grant…may I call you Grant?"

Grant inclined his head. "Of course, you may."

I smiled and nodded. "Well, Grant, I've never been here before. I was hoping to surprise Damien, but I'd probably get lost without your help."

"He's on the top floor." Grant walked me to the office directory and explained the path I needed to take to get to Damien.

"Thank you!" I headed towards the elevator and pushed the button for the twentieth floor. The ride up felt like a lifetime and my stomach was so tied up in nervous knots that I wouldn't be surprised if I lost my lunch in here.

The elevator finally stopped, and I stepped out into one of the most sophisticated office areas I'd ever seen…and into my future.

CHAPTER 24

It's her or it's nothing.

Damien ~

I looked around the prison that was my office-because work was the only thing keeping me from kidnapping the fuck out of Fiona-and wondered how the fuck things got so out of hand. After fucking Fiona until she collapsed, I had made the drive home just to give myself some time to get myself under control. I knew I couldn't keep her in orgasmic bliss 24 hours a day, so I had to come up with some way to make this shit right.

I called Will and had asked him what I should do, and his uncomplicated advice had been to just throw myself on her sword and beg forgiveness. He also had the nerve to tell me that I was wrong about Jason, but then he'd never live his life for only one woman. Still, I had gotten my satisfaction when I had mentioned how Vicky had taken Jason home and had taken care of him. Will seemed to be irritated but had insisted that his night with Vicky had been casual. I knew better, though.

I was so lost in thought that I almost didn't hear the faint knock on my office door. I was pretty sure I was the only one left in the building, but since I hadn't left my office since three this afternoon, I couldn't be sure. It was probably the cleaning service. "Come in." They could just clean around me.

I looked up at the door opening and it's a good thing I was sitting because my knees might have given out on me. "Fiona?" Her steps into my office were hesitant and unsure and I hated that. I stood up and practically ran around my desk to greet her.

I ran my hands up her arms and placed them on her shoulders, peering down at her. She looked scared and...sad. I could handle scared. It was the sad that was fucking me up all to hell. "What are you doing here? Are you okay? Did something happen?" The look on her face was killing me. I searched her precious brown eyes, and all I saw was sad insecurity and it almost brought me to my knees. "Baby, tell me what's wrong?"

And then without any ceremony or any finesse whatsoever, she blurted out the words I'd been waiting to hear since the day she had wanted to share her crayons with me. "I love you."

I knew I heard her correctly, but to be fair, the question needed to be asked, all things considering. "Are you okay, Halloween? Did you hit your head, maybe?"

She let out the most beautiful laugh. "No. I didn't hit my head, you dork."

I bent at the knees and took her face in my hands. I needed a direct view to her face to know for sure. "You love me?"

She looked so worried. "Yeah," she whispered. "I… I do."

I was trying to be happy with what she was giving me, but it wasn't enough. To be honest, even if she gave me everything she had, I still didn't think it'd ever be enough. I quickly flashed back to the threat of tattooing my name on the inside of her thighs. "I can't tell you what it does to me to hear you say you love me, Halloween, but I need you to be *in* love with me." You would think I'd be happy with what she was already giving me, but I was selfish when it came to Fiona. I wanted every molecule that made up her mind, body, and soul.

She gave me a small smile before she clarified. "I love you, Damien. I'm *in* love with you. I have to be. That's the only thing that explains why I keep coming back, no matter what you do to me."

I winced. I couldn't help it. Still, I never regretted my actions, and I'd be lying if I said I did now. I didn't. I'll never regret a single choice I've made because that would mean I was capable of taking another path, and I wasn't. I'm not.

And now that I had her-*really* had her-I'll be dead before I let her go or let someone try to take her from me. "I can't say I'm sorry for any of it, Fiona. I know you deserve an apology and I know I should feel bad for a lot of the things I put you through, but I just don't. I was mean and manipulative because I didn't know how to handle the way you made me feel. You think I tormented you every day, but it was you who tortured the *fuck* out of me every minute of every goddamn day, Halloween." Truth be told, she still tormented me. Her very being was the source of my existence.

Her eyes spilled over and I just prayed they were happy tears as I continued, "There was never a moment in my life where you weren't the only option. Regretting my choices or being sorry would imply that there was, and that's simply not true."

Fiona wrapped her delicate hands around my wrists. "You can't hurt me anymore, Damien." I nodded in earnest, but she kept going. "You can't lie to me or threaten the people I love. You just can't. I love you so much, but the trust isn't coming so easily, so just please, please promise me."

I could only promise her one of those things, and in promising that, I couldn't promise her the other two. "I promise to never lie to you ever again, by outright or by omission. But because I can't promise never to threaten your family or your friends, I can't promise to never hurt you because I know threatening the people you care about would hurt you."

Hey eyes were imploring. *"Why?"*

I stood to my full height and wrapped my arms around her, hugging her to me. "In case you haven't noticed by now, Halloween, I'll do anything to be with you. And now that you've come here and given yourself to me, I'll do anything to keep you. If…if I have to ruin everyone around you to keep you with me, I'll do it."

"Damien…"

"I know a lot of people will say that forcing someone to be with you isn't real love. There's all that nonsense about if you love something set it free and all that shit, and that if you really love a person, you should put their happiness above your own and whatever." I held her tighter. "And maybe that's true for some people, but not me. I'm going to love you like my life depends on it, because it does, Fiona."

I felt her small arms encircle my waist and hug me back. I couldn't stop my mind from wondering where the nearest jewelry store was and if they were still open. Then the more savage part of me imagined her bleeding as I sliced her wide open, yanking that goddamn birth control insert out of her arm. The picture turned more gruesome as I imagined fucking her raw and cumming inside her as she still bled from her arm.

Fuck.

Fiona surrendering to me was supposed to ease the madness, not drive it up ten notches.

I bent down, and grabbing her by her thighs, wrapped them around me, then walked over to sit in my chair. Once I sat down, I adjusted her legs, so that she was sitting sideways across my lap, her legs draped over mine. I had one arm wrapped around her back and the other wrapped around her thigh, holding her to me. I knew I was on the extreme side of crazy when it came to Fiona, but if I could just have her sit right here, Monday through Friday, curled up against me like this, I'd never have a bad day at work.

Fiona brought me out of my irrational thoughts as she sat up. "Um, what's that?"

I tilted my head around her to see what she was talking about. "What?"

She stretched her body to reach over and pluck her picture off my desk. She held it in her hands as she looked down at it, realizing what it was. She lifted her head to look at me. "This is from the day I opened Fiona's."

"I know."

"You've had this on your desk for two years?" she asked incredulously.

"Yep," I answered and thought I might as well tell her all of it. "Open it."

She slid her eyes towards me. "Open it?"

"Yeah, open the little prongs on the back."

She looked back down at the picture frame, turned it over, then opened up the back. She let out a small gasp as three other pictures slid out from behind the visible one. She set the frame back on the desk and shuffled through the pictures.

The first one was of her on our graduation night dressed in her cap and gown. "That one sat on the dresser by my bed when Will and I shared our condo during college." She moved that picture to the back and studied the second photo. It was a closeup of her face going into Mercury's on her twenty-first birthday. "That one was on your twenty-first birthday. You and Vicky were heading into Mercury's. That one sat on my desk in my very first G&C office." She moved on to the third picture. It was of her college graduation, and she was, again, dressed in a cap and gown. This time when she looked up at me, tears were streaming down her face. "That one sat on my desk until the day you opened Fiona's, then it was replaced by the current one."

She quietly put the pictures and frame back together and place it back on my desk. She wiped her face of any remaining tears. Then I laughed at her next words. "You said you didn't have a PI on me until after you left my bedroom that night. Where did the graduation picture come from?"

I kissed the side of her head. "That was a pleasant surprise. Will took it without me even knowing about it. He gave it to me the first night in our condo hoping it would calm me." I shrugged. "And it did."

She rearranged herself, so that she was straddling me, and then she wrapped her arms around my neck, looking me dead in my face. "You can have any woman you want. I have trouble understanding why you want me."

I moved my hands from her hips and tightened my arms around her. "You have what no one else has, and that's my soul. I don't know how to make you truly understand, but you've had it since we were five. I keep telling you, and telling you, but I don't know how else to make you see how serious my need for you is." I leaned in and kissed the corner of her mouth. "Fiona, I can say with absolute certainty that I will never want anyone but you. Hell, I can't even *see* past you to notice any other women. I'll live on my knees in front of you if that's what you need to believe me."

She didn't say anything. Instead, she turned her head to meet my kiss. I just had her yesterday, but it felt as if it's been ages. "I don't know how I get through the hours not being able to touch you, baby."

She pulled back and started trailing kisses down my neck. "I feel the same."

I groaned, and fisting a chunk of her hair, I brought her mouth back to mine. Anyone that can dismiss a kiss as no big deal has never been kissed by their soul mate. I could kiss Fiona forever.

I felt her working on the buttons of my dress shirt and the image of her spread out on my desk before me had my hands shooting straight for the button on her jeans.

She stopped me. "Nu uh. In my office, it was all about me. In your office, it's going to be all about you."

My dick hardened to the point of being painful.

She unbuttoned my shirt completely as she crawled her way down my lap and onto the floor in front of me. Fiona was on her knees in front of me, getting ready to suck my dick, and I didn't know if I'd ever be able to get any work done in this room ever again.

She quickly worked my belt, my button, and then my zipper before running her hand up and down my cock over my boxer briefs. The outline of my dick left no doubt to how much I wanted her. She looked up at me. "How do you want it?"

I almost stuttered my answer because I was so fucking ready for her. "However you want to swallow me, baby."

And then she fucked me all up. "I don't want to swallow you, Damien. I want you to choke me with your cock. I want you to *use* me. I want you out of control. I want you to always want me so badly that you can't control yourself."

I knew that was her insecurities talking, but fuck me, I didn't care. I'd give it to her anyway she wanted if that's what I needed to do to ease her doubts about me needing her. "You want me to fuck that hot mouth of yours, Halloween?"

She already had my cock out, and she gave it one long, smooth lick from the base to the head before answering, "Mmmhmm. I want to do to you what you do to me every time you touch me, Damien."

Fuck, she had no idea.

I spread my legs farther apart to make enough room for her. I didn't bother with pushing my pants down because she couldn't get the entire length of my cock down her throat anyway. Believe me, I've already tried all the other times she's sucked me dry.

I tangled my hand in her hair, then fisting enough of it to where she couldn't escape my hold, I closed my eyes, rested my head backwards, and waited until I felt those soft lips of her close around me. The second she did, I pushed her head down and fucked her mouth like I would her pussy had she been riding me.

I could feel her tongue play with the underside of my cock, teasing the sensitive ridge every time I pulled her head up by her hair. "Fuck yeah, baby."

Her sexy moans grew deeper the more I tried to choke her airways. She was swallowing me like it was her favorite thing in the world to do; like I was her favorite desert.

I swear to God, the biggest struggle I had in life was whether I should shoot my load down her throat or coat her face with it. I could make million-dollar deals in investments with no hesitation, whatsoever, but deciding how she should take my seed always seemed like a battle.

When Fiona cupped my sack and started massaging, I finally decided. "I'm going to shoot everything I have down your throat, baby, and I want you to swallow every last fucking drop."

She started picking up her pace and the tight heat from her mouth along with those little sounds she was making had me on the edge. Fuck, her mouth was exquisite, but I had a feeling a simple hand job from this woman would still have me out of my mind with desire.

"That's it, baby. Suck my cock. Take as much of it as you can. Fuck, Fiona." I tightened my hold in her hair and started making her choke and gag, and it was like a fucking symphony to my ears. "Fuck yeah, baby." I had to close my eyes against the sensation.

I could feel the telltale tingles and could feel the head of my cock expand inside her mouth just before I let out a roar and poured myself down her throat. *"Fuuuuuuck…"*

Fiona stayed at my feet and licked my cock clean until I couldn't take the sensitivity of it any longer. When I finally opened my eyes, I looked down, and she had the biggest satisfied smile on her face. Even on her knees before me, this woman was more powerful than I would ever be.

CHAPTER 25

It's not like any love I know, but I'll take it.

Fiona ~

I chose to believe him.

I chose happiness.

I chose *my* happiness.

While I could admit that the way he loved was intense and often suffocating, I wondered if it felt suffocating because I had been fighting it and him for so long.

Some people may find the idea of his obsession scary, but I didn't. Call me stupid, but I wanted a love that was all-consuming. I wanted to know-not believe or think-but *know* that in a room full of beautiful women, Damien was going to only see me. I wanted a guarantee and I felt like I had it.

We had left his office minutes after I had swallowed him, and now we were sitting in the kitchen bar in his penthouse, eating left over enchilada casserole.

"Can I ask you something?"

He put his fork down and turned to face me. "Anything."

"How is this supposed to work?" I put my fork down, too.

His brow furrowed. "What do you mean?"

"I mean, are we going to only see each other on the weekends? How do we do the long-distance thing?"

He looked amused. "Long-distance thing? Fiona, we only live an hour away from each other."

"Yeah, but the commute time makes it long-distance, Damien." The idea of seeing him on the weekends only was depressing.

"Listen to me and listen very carefully. I will do anything I have to in order to be with you, and if that means driving six hours a day to and from work, I'll do it."

"Damie-"

"No, Fiona. I finally have you and you're out of your mind if you think I'll spend even one night away from you. To hell with that shit," he stressed.

"Maybe we could trade off. Like alternate days where you come see me, and then I come see you."

He was already shaking his head before I even finished. "There is no way I will risk you driving in Bay Area traffic. Nope, not happening, Halloween."

"Oh, but it's okay for you?"

He looked like he was about to get sexist, but he blew me away instead his with reply. "I'm willing to compromise on the driving, but only if you do something for me first."

Holy fuck, Damien Greystone was compromising with me. "Okay, what?"

Damien stood up, grabbed me by my hips, then lifted me to sit on the counter. I had to push the plates back if I didn't want an ass full of enchilada casserole. Once he was standing comfortably in between my spread thighs, he took my face in his hands, then blew me away for the second time in a matter of seconds. "Marry me, Fiona."

My eyes widened to the point of strain. "*Marry you?* We've only been together for a couple of weeks and most of that time was spent fighting or in bed," I pointed out.

The corner of his mouth lifted in a smirk. "Oh, c'mon, like you didn't know that's where this was going to lead?"

My arms started flailing about in exasperation. "Well, yeah…but, I mean, I figured like years later."

He snorted. "Please. I've wanted to marry you since I pulled you away from that tool, Phillip Jansen, at our first school dance."

He was still able to floor me when he said things like that. "I hope you know you ruined my first dance, you jerk."

Damien actually laughed at me. "Jesus, Halloween. It amazes me sometimes that you never caught on. Baby, I was going to ruin all your firsts if they weren't with me." He shrugged a shoulder. "I honestly didn't think Phillip-or *any* guy-would have been stupid enough to approach you. Had I known, I would have gotten to the dance earlier."

As stupid as it sounded all these years later, his comment still hurt my feelings. "Look, I know I was fat and not anything to look at, but I really thought Phillip was my first chance at having a boyfriend and you totally ruined that."

"Whoa, whoa, whoa, wait up. What do you mean you were fat and not anything to look at?" His face looked thunderous, and his voice dripped icicles.

My childhood insecurities made my voice low. "Well, no boy ever asked me out or even really talked to me, so I just thought-"

"Oh, baby." Damien pulled me into him and kissed my forehead. "I'm such an asshole."

"Uh, if you're expecting an argument from me on that, well-"

He chuckled. "I wasn't." He pushed back from me and took my face in his hands again. "Fiona, the reason boys didn't ask you out was because they were too scared."

Too scared?

"Baby, I was always stupid over you, but when you started growing curves and filling out, it was a miracle I hadn't ended up in an insane asylum," he said. "You had the body of a grown fucking woman and every boy in school could see it. It took me beating the fuck out of at least four guys before the entire school realized how serious shit got if any of the guys mentioned your name or showed any interest in dating you."

I knew I shouldn't be shocked anymore, especially considering all that he's already confessed, but, Jesus, what the hell? "So, you're the reason I never had a boyfriend?"

He nodded. "I'm lucky I didn't end up in prison for murdering that stupid fuck Dennis Franks that night he was drunk enough to think he could touch you." He closed his eyes as if he were reliving his emotions from that night all over again. And when he opened them back up, I could actually see the pain reflected in them. "God, Halloween, when it hit me that he was your first actual kiss, I truly wanted to murder the motherfucker. All your firsts were supposed to belong to me. I got too confident and let Dennis slip by me."

"You're nuts, you know that?"

He leaned down and kissed me lightly on the lips. "Yep, I'm very aware. However, instead of tattooing my name all over your body, maybe I need to tattoo yours on mine, and then maybe you'll finally start to believe me when I tell you it's only ever been you since the very first memories of my life."

My heart melted. "I like your tattoos," I confessed.

He raised a brow. "Oh, yeah?"

"You're the most beautiful man I've ever seen. You have to know that only you make me feel like my body's on fire."

He slammed his lips down on mine and kissed me like he wanted to consume me. Suddenly, he broke the kiss and fled from the kitchen, leaving me sitting on the counter light-headed and confused.

Almost immediately, he returned holding some papers and something else I couldn't quite make out. He set the items on the counter next to me and that's when I saw the box.

This man was crazy, and not in the 'oh, you so crazy' way, but in the 'needs to be officially diagnosed' crazy way. I sat there wondering if insanity was hereditary as he opened the box and pulled out an obvious engagement ring.

It was absolutely beautiful.

It was either white gold or platinum with a small diamond surrounded in emeralds. The stones matched his eyes perfectly. "Damien, it's stunning."

Without asking or getting down on one knee or anything, he simply grabbed my left hand and slipped the ring on. It felt a little snug, but it finally made its way over my knuckle. "Are you sure you like it? I can get you another one, maybe with a bigger diamond or something."

His voiced sounded unsure, and I was shocked when I looked up and saw a very nervous and insecure Damien Greystone. "It's perfect. Why would you want to buy another one?"

And as if I couldn't love him more, I found out that I could. "I bought that for you the day I left for Yale. It was very expensive at the age of eighteen when most of my money was tied to my parents. But now that I have my own money, I can get you something bigger if-"

"No!" I shrieked. "Damien it's perfect," I assured him. After I saw him physically relax, I grabbed the papers off the counter. "What are these?"

"Marriage license and all that jazz. You just need to sign, and we can find someone to marry us in the morning," he stated, all matter of fact.

My eyes surely bugged out of my head this time. "Are you craz-" I shook my head. "Never mind."

He laughed.

The jackhole.

"Damien we can't get married tomorrow. We've barely-"

"I've loved you my whole life, and if right now you don't see the rest of your life with me in it, then I'll concede to a long engagement and give you time. But tell me…when you picture your life fifty years from now, do you picture it with me?" he asked.

I couldn't lie and I wouldn't, even if I thought I could. "I see you in everything I'll ever do from this day forward, Damien," I whispered.

He tangled his hands in my hair and brought my lips to his in a soul-claiming kiss. "I love you, Fiona, more than you will ever be able to understand. I'm going to love you every day of my life and every day of my next one."

I gave him a sheepish grin. "You gotta pen?"

He raced around the kitchen pulling open random drawers until he came across one with a pen, and then he threw it at me.

No…you didn't misunderstand that. He *legit* threw it at me.

I was able to catch it, even though I was laughing so hard that I almost fell off the counter. I signed all his documents wondering if my signature would be valid. I was laughing so much that my signature didn't quite look authentic.

My laughter dwindled when I saw how serious his face was. "What's wrong?"

His brows drew inward. "You signed the prenup without even skimming through the pages."

I flapped my hand at him like I was shooing away a fly. "I didn't need to. Everything you have, you've accomplished without any help from me. You should be able to leave the marriage with everything you entered into it with." I lifted a shoulder. "Besides, it's not like I'm starving or anything."

Damien picked up the prenup and flipped through the pages until he found what he was looking for. "Here, read it."

I rolled my eyes and let out a sigh. "Dami-"

"Just read it. *Please.*"

I took the document out of his hands, began reading, and then I really almost did fall off the counter. I snapped my head up, and it was like I was having an out-of-body experience. "You are certifiably insane. Just when I think I've reached the bottom of your crazy, you amaze me with just how much more cracked in the head you seem to be."

"Can we go back to where you just tell me you love me?"

"Damien! I'm serious!"

"So was I," he mumbled under his breath.

I started slapping his chest with the prenup papers. "This states that in the event of a divorce that I get everything. Are you fucking *high?* Do you do drugs? Is that it?"

The asshole really started laughing at me after that.

I started pushing at him. "Get away from me."

"Wait, Halloween, just wait a sec." I turned my head away from him as I crossed my arms over my chest. "Awe, baby, don't be mad. We're getting married tomorrow. Let's not go to bed angry."

"Sarcasm? Seriously?"

He started nibbling soft, sweet kissing down my neck. "Fiona, if we ever get a divorce, it'll be because I did something so horrible that you could no longer love me or live with me. If that happens, you deserve everything I have."

"Dam-"

"Shh, baby, here's the thing. I *know* I'll never do anything to make you want to leave me, so it's not really as big a risk as you think it is." He finished with the kisses and brought his emerald stare to meet my wet one. "We're going to be forever, Fiona. We were always going to be forever."

I let Damien take me to bed and every touch, every kiss, every word was better than I ever thought it could be.

My heart, my mind, and my soul were all finally settled.

I laid in bed, wrapped up in Damien's arms as the steady sound of his breathing filled my ears. I was exhausted, but too excited to fall asleep.

I was getting married tomorrow to a man who I never knew as a girl would come to mean everything to me. The boy with the dark hair and fiery green eyes. The boy who made me cry because he didn't know how to love me. The boy who engulfed my childhood was now the man who was promising me forever.

I may still feel unsure every now and again, but at least I will be able to look back and know that I didn't miss out on the love of my life because I was scared.

I snuggled closer to Damien, and closing my eyes, I fell asleep thinking I couldn't wait to see Vicky kick his ass when I tell her he made me marry him without her.

EPILOGUE

Damien ~

I told Fiona she didn't need to make a big deal out of it, but, as always, she didn't listen.

After about five years of marriage, she had finally started getting a grasp on how much she meant to me, and so she had started getting braver and braver over the years. I've said it before and I'll say it again, she is always her most magnificent when she's showing her backbone.

It didn't help that the kids knew she was my kryptonite, either. They worked as a little team to wrap me around their fingers. I never minded it, though. As long as Fiona was happy, all was right in my world. I had to chuckle when I'd think about the few times the kids would upset her or disappoint her. My wrath at them for upsetting their mother had only been unleashed a handful of time before they realized I was serious about my shit when it came to my wife.

I loved my kids very much, but if you asked my children who I loved more, them or Fiona, they would unanimously say their mother.

Hands-down.

"G-Pop! G-Pop!"

I turned around just in time to catch my third youngest grandson in my arms. We may be celebrating my sixtieth birthday, but I didn't have one foot in the grave just yet. "Hey, Monkey Boy, whatcha doing?" I asked as I placed him on my knee.

"Huero and Boo Boo won't let me play with them and The Girl is boring." I chuckled. Fiona had given me two beautiful healthy kids. We had our daughter, Lucy, who was the oldest and then our son, James, who was the youngest.

Being as fortunate as we were, both kids had been able to go to college and pursue their dreams. James ended up starting at the bottom of G&C, and was now CEO along with Will's oldest son, Brian. He wasn't married yet, but his girlfriend was serious, and she was a sweet, sweet girl. We didn't pressure them, either. We weren't *those* kinds of parents. Whatever made them happy, made us happy.

Lucy had fallen in love and had put her degree in psychology on hold to give us four wonderful grandchildren. Sure, her plan had been to give her husband four beautiful and healthy kids, but they were just parents, we were the grandparents. Our titles held more power. She had every intention of returning to school to finish her degree, but even if she didn't, her husband was solid and took very good care of his family.

Thirty-two years later, our lives were just years, and years of endless blessings, and I never regretted one second of the life I've lived.

"So, what do you want to do since the boys are being meanies and you don't want to play with your sister?"

He wrinkled his little nose. "I can't play with her. She doesn't do anything but sit there and move her arms and legs all over the place. She's boring, G-Pop."

I carried him over to one of the chairs on the patio as I looked out at my family barbecuing, swimming in the pool, and visiting. "Well, she's just a baby, there's not much she can do." Our grandchildren ran the age range of eight, six, four, and three months. Lucy had given us three boys and a baby girl.

"Well, she's still boring," he complained.

"So, what do you want to do?"

He sat in my lap with his little legs dangling over my thighs looking up at me. He looked just like Lucy. "Tell me a story."

"What kind of story? A scary story or a happy story?"

His eyes rounded with the best idea he's had in all his four years of life. "Can you tell me a story that is scary *and* happy?"

I widened my eyes at him. "I sure can."

"Okay, but just tell me. The Brothers can't hear it since they won't let me play with them. This is my story, okay, G-Pop?"

Christ, this kid. I laughed. "Okay, Monkey Boy, this is just your story."

"Okay." He snuggled up to me. "I'm ready."

"Once upon a time, there was this little boy who was sad all the time because he lived in a dark, dark castle. Then one day, he was walking in the woods and he saw a little girl who was so beautiful that she made all the darkness go away. He didn't think she would like him because he was so sad, but she did more than end up liking him. She ended up loving him and protecting him from the darkness."

And she still did.

PLAYLIST

Dollhouse – Melanie Martinez
Saving Me – Nickleback
Back In Black – AC/DC
Beautiful Soul – Jesse McCartney
Animals – Maroon 5
She – Live
The Heart Won't Lie – Reba McEntire
Hysteria – Def Leppard
Standing Still – Jewel
My Love – Justin Timberlake
Pretty Girl – Sugarcult
Right Here – Staind
Take Me To Church – Hozier
Feenin' – Jodeci
Could I Have This Kiss Forever – Whitney Houston
Angel – Aerosmith
Take A Message – Remy Shand
Unwell – Matchbox Twenty
Fallen – Alicia Keys
I Shall Believe – Sheryl Crow
Runaway – Live

ABOUT THE AUTHOR

M.E. Clayton works full-time and writes as a hobby. She is an avid reader and, with much self-doubt, but more positive feedback and encouragement from her friends and family, she took a chance at writing, and the Seven Deadly Sins Series was born. Writing is a hobby she is now very passionate about. When she's not working, writing, or reading, she is spending time with her family or friends. If you care to learn more, you can read about her by visiting the following:

Smashwords Interview

Bookbub Author Page

Goodreads Author Page

OTHER BOOKS

The Seven Deadly Sins Series (In Order)

Catching Avery (Avery & Nicholas)
Chasing Quinn (Quinn & Chase)
Claiming Isabella (Isabella & Julian)
Conquering Kam (Kamala & Kane)
Capturing Happiness

The Enemy Duet (In Order)

In Enemy Territory (Fiona & Damien)
On Enemy Ground (Victoria & William)

The Enemy Series (In Order)

Facing the Enemy (Ramsey & Emerson)
Engaging the Enemy (Roselyn & Liam)
Battling the Enemy (Deke & Delaney)
Provoking the Enemy (Ava & Ace)
Loving the Enemy
Resurrecting the Enemy (Ramsey Jr. & Lake)

The Buchanan Brothers Series (In Order)

If You Could Only See (Mason & Shane)
If You Could Only Imagine (Aiden & Denise)
If You Could Only Feel (Gabriel & Justice)
If You Could Only Believe (Michael & Sophia)
If You Could Only Dream

The How To: Modern-Day Woman's Guide Series (In Order)

How to Stay Out of Prison (Lyrical & Nixon)
How to Keep Your Job (Alice & Lincoln)
How to Maintain Your Sanity (Rena & Jackson)

The Holy Trinity Series (In Order)

The Holy Ghost (Phoenix & Francesca)
The Son (Ciro & Roberta)
The Father (Luca & Remy)
The Redemption (Nico & Mia)
The Vatican (Francisco Phoenix Benetti & Luca Saveria Fiore)

The Blackstone Prep Academy Duet (In Order)

Reflections (Grace & Styx)
Mirrors (London & Sterling)

The Eastwood Series (In Order)
Samson (Samson & Mackenzie)
Ford (Ford & Amelia)
Raiden (Raiden & Charlie)
Duke (Duke & Willow)
Alistair (Alistair & Rory)

The Problem Series (In Order)
The Problem with Fire (Sayer & Monroe)
The Problem with Sports (Nathan & Andrea)
The Problem with Dating (Gideon & Echo)

The Pieces Series (In Order)
Our Broken Pieces (Mystic & Gage)
Our Cracked Pieces (Rowan & Lorcan)
Our Shattered Pieces (Molly & Grayson)

The Holy Trinity Duet (In Order)
The Bishop (Leonardo & Sienna)
The Cardinal (Salvatore & Blake)

The Holy Trinity Next Generation Series (In Order)
Vincent & Cira (Vincent Fiore & Cira Benetti)
Salvatore Jr. & Camilla (Salvatore Benetti Jr. & Camilla Mancini)
Emilio & Bianca (Emilio Benetti & Bianca Mancini)
Angelo & Georgia (Angelo Benetti & Georgia Mancini)
Dante & Malia (Dante Fiore & Malia Benetti)
Mattia & Remo (Mattia Mancini & Remo Vitale)

The Rýkr Duet (In Order)
Avalon (Avalon & Griffin)
Neve (Neve & Easton)

Standalone
Unintentional
Purgatory, Inc.
My Big, Huge Mistake
An Unexpected Life
The Heavier the Chains…
Real Shadows
You Again
Dealing with the Devil

Printed in Great Britain
by Amazon